Return to Alcatraz

Also by Tina Westbrook

Letters from Alcatraz
Forty Years Later

Return to Alcatraz

Tina Westbrook

Order this book online at www.trafford.com
or email orders@trafford.com

Most Trafford titles are also available at major online book retailers.

Photography provided by: Tina Westbrook and Janice Fife.
Author photo provided by John Catelli

Printed in the United States of America.

ISBN: 9781426943577 (sc)
ISBN: 9781426943560 (hc)
ISBN: 9781426943584 (e)

Our mission is to efficiently provide the world's finest, most comprehensive book publishing service, enabling every author to experience success. To find out how to publish your book, your way, and have it available worldwide, visit us online at www.trafford.com

Trafford rev. 09/18/2010

www.trafford.com

North America & international
toll-free: 1 888 232 4444 (USA & Canada)
phone: 250 383 6864 • fax: 812 355 4082

For John Catelli:

You are a constant source of inspiration.

Acknowledgement`s

First and foremost, I must thank John Catelli, aka Mr. Alcatraz, for his love and friendship. His stories continue to spark my imagination.

My husband David – Thank you for supporting me on this journey. I love you.

To my daughter Tiffany and my son-in-law Tommy, I owe a special debt of gratitude. Thank you both so much for all the effort you put forth in making *Letters from Alcatraz* a success. I hope you don't mind doing it again!

Jared Goldstein at Turnaround Media – I am fortunate to have you in my corner. Thank you for all that you have done.

To the staff at Trafford Publishing: Thank you for your professionalism and the spirit in which you operate. Through all the emails and telephone conversations, you always leave me with a smile.

To the staff at Alcatraz and all the volunteers at Alcatraz Gardens - each and every one of you are special. Your love for Alcatraz shines through and I thoroughly enjoyed the time I spent there.

To Janice Fife – Thank you for being the best sister a girl could ever hope for (even though we do have different parents). And a special thanks for providing photographs for this project. I love you!

And a special thanks to Jay Stafford. You are always there to lend an ear and encourage me in a way that words truly can't explain; even when I'm being my neurotic self. I love you dearly.

Return to Alcatraz

Prologue

With the sun barely peeking through the clouds I made my way to Pier 33. This city that I once loved was now a place I didn't want to be. It took a mere five days to not only change the way I saw San Francisco, but to change the way I saw people. My entire attitude toward life had changed and I felt that I had aged twenty years.

I thought about the time I spent with C.J. and a smile crept up on my face. I knew that C.J. was special; a kind man with a smile that I would always remember. He has a way of reaching into one's heart and not letting go. It was easy to understand why women flocked to him and I no longer found myself wondering how he was able to do that. People similar to C.J. seem to get through life using their looks to get what they want, but with C.J. it was different. He had charisma and it occurred to me that that was a rare quality these days.

I thought about Chuck and no matter how hard I tried I was unable to figure him out. At first glance it was apparent that he inherited his father's good looks, but his attitude and personality definitely came from somewhere else. I didn't like Chuck and after spending five days in San Francisco it was obvious that Chuck didn't like me either.

After all the letters I had received from C.J. I assumed I knew virtually all there was to know about him, but I had been wrong in my assumption. People are more than what they write in a few e-mail messages. They have lives, families and histories. I now know that it's our life experiences that make us who we are. I understood how C.J. became the man he became, but I wondered how Chuck became the man he came to be. What was it that happened in his life that made him so angry?

When it came to Chuck, C.J. had only one thing to say, *"It's good that he speaks his mind. Both he and Bella were raised to think for themselves, and whether I agree or disagree with their opinions, I respect them."* I wondered if C.J. really felt that way, or if it was the polite thing to say about one's own child. After much consideration I concluded that he really did feel that way.

Arriving at Pier 33 I glanced around and there he was; leaning up against the wall of Alcatraz Landing Café. My eyes shifted to the ground and I saw the shoebox. Chills ran down my spine and I momentarily considered running the other way. I wasn't sure whether or not I wanted it. Somehow I had the feeling that I was about to open Pandora's box and that may not be a good thing. Not that I wasn't interested in the contents of that box, but more because this family had taken an emotional toll on me and I wasn't quite sure how much more I could take.

I slowly approached him and when he noticed me he bent down and picked up the box. No words were spoken. The box was placed in my hands and I turned away.

One

My eyes darted across the dock and I feared that C.J. had already left. I couldn't imagine he would leave so abruptly, but just yesterday I couldn't have imagined that I would be attending Diana's memorial service either.

"Tina! Over here!"

I knew that voice! I turned to my left and saw C.J. waving his hand. Relief set in as I walked toward the group that surrounded him. Then I saw Chuck. I had caught Chuck staring me down several times throughout the service, but I managed to avert my attention elsewhere. Chuck not only seemed confused by my presence, but he also seemed angry.

"Tina, I just wanted to tell you how much it meant to me to have you here today. I must run now, but I will be in touch. When do you head home?"

I took a deep breath and told C.J. that I would be heading home in a couple of days. Then I asked if I could speak with him for a moment. My heart was racing and I knew I couldn't let C.J. leave until my mind was at ease.

"Of course my dear, let's go for a walk!" C.J. shook hands with those surrounding him, kissed a few ladies on the cheek, and then told Chuck he would be back shortly. Chuck just continued to stare me down.

As C.J. and I began to walk away from the crowd he placed his hand in mine. As our fingers wrapped themselves around each other I realized that I was squeezing his hand rather tightly, but I couldn't stop myself and I didn't want to let go.

"C.J., I need to know that you're okay. I'm worried about you and I want to talk to you. Is there any possible way that we can get together this evening or perhaps in the morning?" I knew I was taking a risk by asking him this, but if something happened to him I knew I would never be able to forgive myself for not taking that risk.

C.J. turned to face me and with his eyes staring directly into mine he told me that there was no need to worry. What bothered me was the fact that he wouldn't agree to meet with me.

"C.J., if there's no need to worry then will you promise me that we'll talk soon?"

C.J. smiled and kissed me on the forehead. "Tina my dear, I promise you that you have not heard the last from me! I will be in touch. I hate to take off like this today, but there are things that I must tend to. Please enjoy your day and know that I am okay; I promise you that."

I still felt uneasy and suddenly that all too familiar feeling of doom was creeping back in. I felt helpless and had no idea how I could keep C.J. from leaving. "Okay. I understand. I'll be waiting to hear from you!"

C.J. wrapped his arms around me and whispered in my ear, "I love you." A tear ran down my face and as I tightened my embrace I told C.J. that I loved him too.

Not another word was spoken and I watched C.J. as he walked back to the dock. I noticed Isabella walking toward her father and then I spotted Chuck. It was in that moment that I realized why Chuck had seemed familiar to me as we sat talking on the plane; his resemblance to C.J. was uncanny.

Two

There are few things in life that I regret. I learned long ago that having regrets will get you nowhere. Regrets will trap you. They will prevent you from moving forward. Regrets will keep you locked in a place that you don't want to be. They are useless and a complete waste of time and energy. Unfortunately, knowing all of that doesn't change much. I regret not going back to the hotel immediately following Diana's memorial service. I will regret that for the rest of my life.

The sun was shining brightly and the area was bustling with people; the majority of which I concluded to be tourists. Instead of returning to the Marriott Hotel I decided to take C.J.'s advice; I attempted to enjoy my day.

I momentarily thought about going back to the hotel so that I could grab my camera, but quickly decided that for once I would just take in the sights. Really take in the sights. There are so many things that one misses when viewing the world through the lens of a camera. Photographers get so caught up in getting that "perfect shot" that we tend to spend every moment either looking for that shot, or setting up that shot. In the meantime things are happening all around us and we fail to see most of it; unless of course it's something that we consider to be "photo worthy."

I strolled through Fisherman's Wharf and found myself people watching. People will do some of the funniest things, especially when they don't realize someone is watching them. I had just sat down on a bench when two men caught my eye. It was in that very moment that I completely understood why this is one of C.J's favorite activities.

Directly across from where I was sitting I watched as two city employees sat down and began to pass a joint back and forth. It was apparent that they had no concern for the mere fact that they were in a very public place. Nor did they seem concerned with the fact that what they were doing was illegal or that they were city employees on duty. They seemed absolutely oblivious to where they were, or perhaps it was just a temporary lapse in judgement. In spite of it all, I found the situation to be rather amusing. I reasoned that San Francisco could quite possibly be the only place in the United States where one would witness such an act in broad daylight in one of the most popular tourist locations in the state.

After spending a fair amount of time people watching hunger pains hit me and I went on the search for something good. Not good for me, but good! I had an intense craving for a cheeseburger and fries and I finally found just the right place to indulge my craving. It was a small little hole in the wall, but it smelled so good that I walked right in and placed my order.

As I enjoyed my, oh so good, but not so good for me lunch, my thoughts returned to C.J. I don't know if it was intuition or paranoia that was kicking in, but the more I thought about C.J. the more worried I became. I finished my lunch and then I failed to do the one thing that I always tell people to do; listen to that internal voice!

I left the restaurant and although every fiber of my being was telling me to go back to the hotel, I instead opted for some retail therapy. I browsed one little shop after another and when I finally checked my watch I discovered that it was nearing 5pm. Exhausted from the day's events I headed back to the Marriott.

I searched my purse, I searched my luggage, and I suddenly felt myself being overcome with desperation and fear. I sat down on the edge of the bed and I read C.J's letter again.

My Dearest Tina,

As I sit here writing to you I find myself struggling for the words. For you are the one person I have been able to open up with completely, yet what I need to say to you seems impossible.

I fear that you will not understand and more than that, I fear that you may somehow place blame on yourself.

I have told you my story and in the process you have come to comprehend the love that I have for my wife. I have always known that losing Diana was not an option. I have methodically prepared myself for this day and know now that I am ready.

Once we leave Alcatraz I will take the final steps in my year long journey. I have prepared letters for Chuck and Isabella and I pray that they will someday understand why I couldn't stay.

Although my journey has come to an end, your journey is just beginning. What I am leaving to you is the one item that has kept me going. It has been my lifeline for a year. Once it is in your hands you will discover, as I did, the love of a woman.

Tina, saying goodbye is never easy, but we must all say goodbye at some point in time. I trust you will know what to do.

May your guardian angel always watch over you.

Much love,
C.J.

It was as if a light bulb went off in my head and I remembered where I placed the phone number that Chuck had given me. I made a quick dash to the in room safe and removed my file folder.

I dialed the number and waited for him to answer. The phone rang seven times before I heard Chuck's voice.

"Hello?"

"Chuck? It's Tina."

There was a long pause and then Chuck cleared his throat. "What do you want?"

I took a deep breath and with tears running down my face I attempted to explain. "Chuck, I need your fathers address. I have called him at home several times and he's not answering. I tried to get his address from information, but his phone number is unpublished, so the operator will not give me it to me. I need to talk to him as soon as possible."

There was a long, almost deafening silence. I thought Chuck may slam down the phone and I didn't want that to happen, so I spoke up again. "Chuck, I know you're upset right now. I know you don't understand, and I'm sure your father will explain all of this to you, but right now I need to speak with him."

Chuck cleared his throat again and in a near whisper he told me that he had not spoken to C.J. since the service. "I asked him if he wanted to go to lunch, or maybe head over to the house so we could catch up on things, but he told me that he had some things to do and that we would have to catch up later."

I didn't want to hear that. I needed to speak with C.J. and I knew it couldn't wait. "Chuck, I really need your fathers address. He is here in San Francisco, isn't he?"

"Yes Tina. He's in San Francisco, but I'm not going to give you his address. I would imagine if he wanted you to have his address he would have given it to you himself."

"Chuck, listen to me…you don't understand. It's imperative that I speak with C.J. and I need to speak with him tonight."

"Why? What's so important that it won't keep? I don't get it. What the fuck is the deal between the two of you? Why do you need to talk to him tonight? He didn't even want to talk to his own children tonight. What makes you think he wants to talk to you?"

"Chuck, he may not want to talk to me tonight, but I want to talk to him."

"Oh, and I'm suppose to just give you his address so you can show up at his door? No thanks. I'm going to take a pass on that."

I was stunned and panic was taking over. I tried to figure out what I could say that would persuade Chuck to help me out, but I couldn't come up with anything. Before I could get another word out Chuck chimed back in.

"I'll tell you what I'll do. I'll come back out there. I'll pick you up and I will take you to dads, but on the way there you're going to have to tell me what's going on. Take it or leave it."

I tried to imagine the look on C.J's face if Chuck and I showed up on his doorstep, but if this was my only option then I wasn't going to turn it down.

"Fine, I'll take it. I'm at the Fisherman's Wharf Marriott. What time will you be here?"

"I'm in Oakland, so give me at least an hour. Tina, I swear to God, if you don't tell me what the fuck's going on I will turn the damn car around and take you back. Do you understand?"

Sitting in the lobby waiting for Chuck was mentally excruciating. I was trying to decide what I would tell him about his father and what I absolutely would not tell him. That damn feeling of doom was hanging over my head like a black cloud. Then without warning I began to contemplate whether going to C.J's was such a good idea after all.

I looked at my watch and scanned the lobby for the umpteenth time; *what is taking so long?* It had been nearly two hours since I spoke with Chuck. I sat there contemplating whether or not I should just call the police. As I stood up to walk outside and dial 911 Chuck walked in.

"My God - What took so long?"

"Hey, gimme a break, traffic was fucking horrendous. I didn't realize that we were on some kind of a time schedule."

The clock on the dashboard noted the time of death; 9pm. That was the last thing I saw. What followed immediately afterward is a blur. I heard a voice - Chuck's voice, but I can't recall what he said. My ears were ringing and I stood paralyzed.

Chuck had been driving like a mad man and as we barreled into C.J.'s driveway he slammed the car into park and jumped out. The car was still running and I looked at the clock. I stepped out of the car and before I could even attempt to shut the car door I heard the unmistakable sound that will forever haunt me. It was the sound of a gunshot; one single shot.

I don't know how long I had been standing there, but it was long enough for C.J.'s neighbors to gather around. A crowd had begun to form and it was as if I were having an out of body experience. I stood there, frozen in my tracks, my ears still ringing. I couldn't move and I could barely breathe. It seemed as if voices were shouting way off in the distance. I heard "911", I heard "C.J.", and I heard crying. Then I realized that the voices I was hearing were my own. I felt a hand grab my arm and I looked up to see Chuck.

"Fuck Tina! Call 911! Jesus Christ!" I watched as Chuck ran toward the back of the house and then I scrambled to grab my cell phone from inside the car.

"911, what's your emergency?"

"I, um, I need an ambulance. No, I need the police."

"What's the problem Ma'am?"

"There's been a shooting. No, I think it's a suicide."

"What address are you calling from?"

"I don't know. I don't know!"

I was frantic and if C.J. weren't already dead I knew time was of the essence. I looked around for an address, but I didn't see a mailbox. I just started screaming, "Where are we? What's the address?"

An older gentleman walked over to me "1392…give me the phone!"

As the man yanked the phone from my hand I spotted Chuck. He was now at the front door and I could hear the echo his fist was making as he pounded against the solid wood. A few men approached Chuck and I watched as they attempted to get him to move away from the door. "My father's in there! Someone help me!" Chuck fell to his knees and a petite elderly woman wrapped her arms around him.

For me, time stood still. It felt like an eternity. I remember feeling a need to comfort Chuck, but I was unable to make my feet leave the spot they were firmly planted on.

The sound of sirens have always left me feeling a bit unnerved, but to hear them in the distance this time felt like a weight was being lifted off my shoulders. I saw the flashing lights and I heard voices telling those on the scene to get out of the way.

I watched as several people wearing uniforms approached the front door. Then I watched as two of them physically pulled Chuck from the porch. My eyes flew wide open when I caught a glimpse of a gentleman exit an unmarked police car. I knew that man. Tony Richter.

The crowd that had been gathered in front of C.J.'s house was now standing on either side of the property. Chuck was standing on the sidewalk and a uniformed police officer was speaking with him. I watched as officers forced their way into the house and then, without warning, Chuck darted toward the porch. Once again he found himself physically restrained. This time they didn't allow Chuck to just stand there waiting. They placed him in the back seat of a police car.

Moments after officers entered C.J.'s house an ambulance arrived. I stood there watching, waiting, and praying. I knew if a stretcher came out with C.J.'s body on it then he was still alive; if not, then I knew the coroner would be called.

"Tina, here's the problem. You knew Mr. Julianno was suicidal, right?"

I looked up at Tony and shook my head. "Tony, C.J. never came right out and told me that he was going to kill himself. I was worried about him."

"That's not what Chuck is saying. He said that you knew. He said that you told him that you received a suicide letter from Mr. Julianno just hours prior to the shooting. Is that true?"

I didn't know how to answer that question and I was trying to remember everything that happened. I sat there in that chair trying to make sense of everything and at the same time I was searching my mental data base.

"Tina, I can only help you if you're honest with me. You need to tell me everything you knew and when you knew it."

"Tony, I don't understand why we're even here. C.J. committed suicide. I didn't kill him. I realize Chuck is upset; he has every reason to be upset, but why am I here?"

Tony cleared his throat and then leaned in closer to me. "Tina, we're here because a man is dead. We're here because a law has been broken…"

"What? What law?"

"Tina, every person who deliberately aids, or advises, or encourages another to commit suicide, is guilty of a felony. That law!"

I suddenly realized that I was in trouble. *Did I aid, or advise or encourage C.J. to commit suicide?* "Tony, if I'm in trouble then I want an attorney. I, in no way, aided, advised or encouraged C.J. to commit suicide."

Tony stood up and walked over to where I was sitting. "Listen to me. I don't know what you knew or what you didn't know. A man is dead. A man you claim to care about. A man, that you flew half way across the country to see, is dead. I need to know, from you, if you knew he was going to commit suicide? That's it Tina. You need to answer that question."

"Tony, I suspected he was contemplating suicide and I made every attempt to talk to him today. My suspicions weren't confirmed until I arrived back at the hotel earlier this evening and found a letter that had been slid under the door. It was at that time that I realized C.J. was planning on killing himself."

"Okay, what did you do after finding the letter?"

"What did I do? I began calling him. After several non-successful attempts to reach him I called Chuck."

"Okay. From the moment you found the letter, to the moment you arrived at Mr. Julianno's home, how much time had passed?"

"I don't know…let me think. I arrived back at the hotel around 5pm. Well, between 5 and 5:30. The letter was in an envelope, lying on the floor, when I entered my room. At first I thought it was a hotel bill, but then I realized it couldn't be since I had a couple more days before my scheduled check out. That's when I opened the envelope and found the letter."

"Okay, so it's around 5:30, you read the letter and did it immediately occur to you that Mr. Julianno was going to commit suicide?"

"My God Tony…I read that letter more than once and my fears that he had been contemplating suicide were now confirmed. Yes, it occurred to me that he was going to attempt suicide."

"And, what did you do next?"

"I tried to call him. I dialed his number, but there was no answer. I tried over and over again, but no answer."

"Then what did you do?"

"I thought about Chuck. No, that's wrong. I didn't think about Chuck. I grabbed the phone book to search for C.J.'s address, but he wasn't listed. Then I dialed information."

"Why were you searching for his address?"

"I was worried about him."

"Go on…what did you do next?"

"Information wouldn't give me his address because his number was unpublished. I didn't know what to do. That's when I thought about Chuck. I remembered that

Chuck had given me his phone number before the plane touched down in San Francisco, so I searched for Chuck's phone number."

Tony ran his hand through his hair and then began to pace the floor. "Did you know that Chuck was Mr. Julianno's son?"

"I didn't before this morning. We were at Diana's memorial service this morning at Alcatraz when C.J. introduced us. Before that moment I had no idea."

Tony shook his head and the look on his face told me that he didn't believe me. I didn't have to wait long for him to express his opinion with words.

"C'mon Tina…let me get this straight. You sat next to Chuck on that plane for six hours and you never knew he was Mr. Julianno's son? Is that right?"

"Yeah Tony, that's right. I also sat next to you on that plane for six hours. Did you know that you would be questioning me about a suicide?"

Tony took a deep breath and sat back down across from me. "Okay, so you called Chuck? Is that right?"

"It took me a little while to find his number. I searched my purse for it, searched my luggage, but it wasn't there. I searched both again and then re-read C.J.'s letter. That's when I remembered where Chuck's phone number was."

"So that's when you called Chuck?"

"Yes."

"Okay. It was during that phone call that you told Chuck you suspected Mr. Julianno was suicidal?"

"No. I asked him for his father's address."

"Did he give it to you?"

"No, he didn't. He refused to give me C.J.'s address. I told him that it was imperative that I get his address, but he wouldn't give it to me."

Once again Tony ran his hand through his hair. "Okay, let me try to understand this. You told Chuck that his father could be suicidal, but Chuck refused to give you the address?"

"No. I didn't tell Chuck that C.J. could be suicidal."

"Why not?"

Why Not? Why didn't I tell Chuck? Oh my God… "I didn't have the chance. Chuck refused to give me the address…instead he told me that he would take me to C.J.'s, but I would have to tell him what was going on or he would turn the car back around."

"Give me a fucking break Tina! You knew Mr. Julianno was suicidal, but you didn't tell anyone? You found the letter between 5 and 5:30 and you arrived at Mr. Julianno's home at what time?"

"It was 9 o'clock when we arrived at C.J.'s and heard the gun shot."

"So you let three and a half hours…4 hours pass before trying to get help?"

"No! I had been trying to get help since finding the letter. What part of what I'm saying do you not understand? If there's anyone to blame for this it's Chuck. If he had just given me C.J.'s address we wouldn't be sitting here right now."

Tony stood back up and then slammed his fist down on the table. "No Tina, it's not Chuck's fault. You knew Mr. Julianno was suicidal, but you let three and a half, four hours pass before doing anything. Let me ask you this: Why didn't you pick up the telephone and dial 911? The moment you received that letter you could have dialed 911. Give the operator Mr. Julianno's phone number and officers would have went to the premises. Why didn't you do that?"

Why didn't I do that? Why didn't I do that? "I didn't think about that until later."

"How much later Tina? When did the thought of dialing 911 finally occur to you?"

"I was in the hotel lobby waiting for Chuck and nearly two hours had passed since I spoke with him. I was beginning to worry that he had changed his mind about taking me to C.J.'s, that's when I thought about dialing 911."

Tony appeared agitated and began pacing the floor again. "I just don't understand. Here's a person you obviously cared about, you came to California...why? Why did you come to California?"

"I came to California because he asked me to."

"Because he asked you to...okay, I still don't get it, but here you are. Then you find a note under your door and you believe he's going to commit suicide, but yet the thought of dialing 911 never enters your mind? Seriously - Is that what you want me to believe?"

"I don't care what you believe. That's the truth."

"Well Darlin', we have a problem. I don't think that's what happened at all. I think you knew Mr. Julianno was going to commit suicide and I think you knew it long before that plane touched down. I think there was a plan and I think you helped Mr. Julianno carry out that plan. Do you seriously think, for one minute, that I believe it was sheer coincidence that you and Chuck arrived at Mr. Julianno's home at the exact moment he pulled the trigger?"

My head was spinning and I felt nauseous. This could not be happening. "I don't really care what you believe! I am telling you the truth! I'm leaving!"

As I stood up to leave Tony grabbed my arm and looked me directly in my eye. "No, I'm afraid you're not leaving. Assisted suicide is a crime and you're under arrest."

Tony walked over to the door and motioned for another officer to come inside the room. Then Tony said the words that I never imagined I would be hearing. "You have the right to remain silent; Anything you say can and will be used against you in a court of law; You have the right to talk to a lawyer and have a lawyer present with you during questioning; If you cannot afford a lawyer, one will be appointed for you if you so desire; If you choose to talk to the police, you have the right to end the interview at any time. Do you understand each of these rights as I have explained them to you? With these rights in mind, do you wish to talk to us now?"

"You know what? Fuck you Tony! You've got this all wrong. And, I asked for an attorney at the beginning of this interview. Remember that? I specifically told you that if I were in any trouble I wanted an attorney, but you just kept asking questions. Now you're arresting me?"

Tony started to walk out of the room and when he reached the door he looked back and muttered two words: "Book her."

Sleep had not been an option that night in the San Francisco County Jail. Immediately after being arrested I was taken to San Francisco County Jail #1. It was there that I was informed that within 24 hours I would be moved to San Francisco County Jail #8, where all female prisoners are housed. It was 2am when I was placed in a cell with six other women. I would have to wait until morning before being permitted to speak with an attorney. Morning could not come quickly enough.

I felt helpless, hopeless and incredibly sad. My mind began to replay the events of the day and I struggled to figure out how I came to be in my current situation.

I thought about C.J., and recalled the moment the stretcher was brought out of the house. I felt relief when I realized that C.J. was still alive, but I also felt immense fear. A sheet had been placed over C.J.'s body and it appeared to be covered in blood. I didn't know if he would survive. I closed my eyes and recalled the events that followed.

"Get in the fuckin' car!"

I looked over and saw Chuck standing next to the driver's side door. "Where are we going?"

"We're following the ambulance to the hospital. If you're going with me then get in the fucking car!"

I sat down in the car and Chuck backed out of the driveway; within seconds we were directly behind the ambulance.

"How could you let this happen?"

I looked over at Chuck and saw tears rolling down his face. "Chuck, I didn't let this happen. How could I have prevented this?"

"You knew he was suicidal. You could have told me that this morning. You could have told me that on the phone this evening. You could have dialed 911. You let this happen! Why?"

I didn't say a word. Instead I just sat there. It was painfully obvious that Chuck blamed me for his father's attempt at suicide and there was nothing I could say to him in that moment that was going to change his mind.

Chuck grabbed his cell phone and began to dial. “Bella… Bella, where are you? Okay. Listen to me. I need you to get to San Francisco General Hospital. No, I’m okay. Bella, I’ll have to explain when you get there. Hurry…its dad. Okay, love you too.”

It was 10:12pm when Chuck slammed the car into park. We both jumped out of the car and ran through the emergency room doors. We were only steps behind the stretcher that carried C.J. and as the stretcher pushed its way through the swinging doors Chuck continued to follow. A nurse stopped him just as he was about to enter. “I’m sorry Sir, you can’t come back here.”

“That’s my father. He’s been shot.”

“Yes sir and we’re going to do everything we can to help him, but I need you to take a seat and fill out some forms for us.”

“Fill out forms? My father may be dying. I’m not going to fill out fucking forms!”

The nurse didn’t say another word. Instead, she placed her arm around Chuck and walked him over to a chair. Chuck sat down and I sat down next to him.

“Ma’am, are you related?”

“No, I’m not. I’m a friend of Mr. Julianno’s.”

“I see. Well, we’re going to need some information. Is there anyone else that can provide it?”

“I believe Mr. Julianno’s daughter is on her way. I’m sure she will be able to provide any information you need.”

The nurse smiled, nodded, and then asked us to let her know once Isabella arrived.

As Chuck and I sat there, in silence, I began to take inventory of those around us. The waiting room was filled to near capacity and I wondered if this was an unusually busy night or if it were always this busy. I almost asked Chuck about the hospitals reputation, but before I had a chance to mumble anything, Chuck stood up. That was when I noticed the man in scrubs facing Chuck.

"Hello. Are you Mr. Julianno's family?"

Chuck shook his head. "I'm his son. Is he okay?"

"Mr. Julianno, if you will come with me please."

Chuck looked at me and reached out his hand. As I stood up and placed my hand in his my thoughts went back to hours earlier when C.J. took me by the hand and told me that he was fine.

The doctor led us down a corridor and then into a small room.

"Mr. Julianno, I'm very sorry to have to tell you this, but your father was dead on arrival."

Chuck let go of my hand and slumped into a chair. "I don't understand. How? He was still alive when he was put in the ambulance. It didn't take us long to get here. How can he be dead? Are you sure? This can't be happening."

My eyes were filling with tears and it didn't take long for them to start falling.

"Mr. Julianno, your father died of a gunshot wound to the head. His injury was fatal. Once he was placed in the ambulance it was only a matter of time. Had he been shot right here in the hospital there would have been nothing we could have done to save his life; I am so sorry. If you would like to see him we can certainly arrange that. We have a chaplain if you would like to speak with him."

Chuck wiped the tears away and then informed the doctor that his sister was on her way; he would wait for her.

"That's fine. Whenever you're ready please let us know." The doctor walked out of the room and Chuck stood back up.

"I hope you know that all of this is your fault. If not for you my father would still be alive."

In that moment I knew there was nothing I could say that would change Chuck's mind or even give him peace at that moment. Looking back at it now, I may have made the wrong decision, but I stood up and walked out of that room. I walked back down the corridor, into the emergency room and out the sliding glass doors.

Once outside I rummaged through my purse until I found my cigarettes and lighter. With shaking hands, I lit a cigarette and wondered how long it had been since I smoked my last. This had been the longest day of my life and I decided that I would call for a taxi and go back to the Marriott.

"Tina?"

I turned around to find Tony Richter standing there.

"Tony! Did you hear? C.J. passed away."

"Yes, I know. I was at his house when the call came in. Tina, I need to speak with you. Chuck made a few statements earlier this evening and he seems to be under the impression that you knew Mr. Julianno was going to commit suicide. Now, I don't know if he's rambling out of grief, or if there's something to what he's saying, but we need to get this cleared up. Would you mind going to the station with me?"

"Tony, I am so tired I can't even see straight. I was hoping to go back to the hotel. I really don't think there's anything I could say that would make Chuck feel any better."

Tony ran his hand through his hair and then moved a bit closer to me. "Probably not, but I need to get your statement."

"Statement? I didn't know y'all took statements when someone kills themselves."

"Well, this doesn't seem like the ordinary, run of the mill suicide. It's not very often that we have the victims son telling us that someone knew it was going to happen, but did nothing to prevent it."

"Is that what he told you? Tony, I did everything I knew to do to help C.J."

Tony smiled and then placed his hand on my shoulder. "I'm sure you did, but we will have to get your statement. So, we can either go to the station right now, or we can talk first thing tomorrow. Which will it be?"

"Well, we might as well go tonight, because tomorrow I'm getting out of this city."

"Jacobs, Lawrence, Morgan, Parish, Roberts, Randall, and Westbrook, let's go Ladies! You have a court appearance to make."

I stood up and glanced over at the woman walking toward me. "I don't understand. What court appearance? I don't even have an attorney yet."

The guard looked at me, slightly smiled and then placed handcuffs on my wrists. "What? Is this your first rodeo?"

"I'm afraid it is. I haven't even been able to make a phone call. I don't know who to call; I don't know what's going on."

"Well, let me try to fill you in. Right now you're going to see the judge. And, when he's done with you you're going to be transferred to the #8 jail. Anything else I can clear up for you?"

She had a smug look on her face and I knew she thought she was better than me. I could actually sense, that because I was the one in handcuffs and she was the one in charge, that she thought she was better than me.

"No. There's nothing else I need you to clear up for me." As she turned away I whispered "Bitch."

Ms. Westbrook, you have been charged with involuntary manslaughter. Do you understand the charges against you?" The judge never looked up from the paper in front of him.

"No, I don't understand. I don't know why I'm here."

The judge raised his eyes and put the paper that he had been reading down. "Ms. Westbrook, you have been charged with involuntary manslaughter. You need to keep in mind that anything you say can be used against you in trial. Now, having said that, is there anything you need to ask me?"

"How do I get an attorney?"

"Can you afford an attorney or do you require a court appointed attorney?"

"I can afford an attorney, but I don't know who to call. I don't live here. Do I get bail?"

"Ms. Westbrook, this is simply a hearing to inform you of the charges against you. A court date will be scheduled and at that time you will be able to enter your plea. Bail has been set at fifty thousand dollars. This amount was set according to a published bail schedule. Bail may be posted at any time."

"But how do I post bail? How do I find an attorney? And when will I be allowed to make a phone call?"

"Ms. Westbrook, holding cells have telephones. The telephone is available for arrestees to make calls to arrange bail, inform family, or to reach the public defender. I would suggest you call someone and have them find you an attorney or look one up in the yellow pages. If you cannot afford an attorney please tell me now; the court will appoint an attorney should you so desire."

"Yes your honor, I understand that, but I have no family in California and the telephones only allow calls within the local dialing area. How do I reach my family if I can't make a long distance telephone call?"

The judge appeared irritated and then in no uncertain terms told me to either call a local attorney, the public defender's office, or make a collect call.

My blood was beginning to boil and I once again felt as if I were being looked down upon. *Just who the fuck do these people think they are?* "Thank you your honor. I understand. I don't need a court appointed attorney; I will find my own."

Once the charges had been formally read to those waiting, we were taken back to the intake and release jail. The same guard that had placed me in handcuffs was now removing them. "Look, I have never been in trouble before. This is all new to me. I need to find an attorney... anyone that you could recommend?"

"Look, it's not my job to help detainee's find a lawyer. Ask some of the people that are in here with you."

I looked around at the group and quickly decided to phone home.

Tina, what the hell is going on?" David sounded really pissed off and for a moment I questioned whether or not calling him had been such a good idea after all.

"I've been arrested and my bail is fifty thousand dollars."

"Fifty thousand dollars - what did you do? When did you get arrested? What happened?"

"Okay, to make a long story short, I was arrested for involuntary manslaughter. I was arrested last night and right now I'm in a holding cell, but I'm about to be transferred to another jail. I need an attorney!"

"Involuntary manslaughter? What the fuck happened?"

"Oh my God…C.J. committed suicide last night."

"What? What happened? If he committed suicide then why are you in jail?"

"They arrested me because they think I knew he was going to do it, but I didn't do anything to stop it. Can you believe that? How do you stop someone from killing themselves?"

David didn't say anything.

"David, I need you to call Jack. Maybe he will know who to call out here. Listen, I need you to post my bail."

"So, um, how am I supposed to do that? Can I just call it in with a credit card?"

I sensed sarcasm in David's voice. "No, I don't think you can do that. Call Jack! Would you just call Jack? If we use a bail bondsman it's only ten percent. We're talking about five thousand dollars. Can you do that?"

"Yeah, I can call Jack. I told you that going out there wasn't a good idea. I told you that I didn't feel good about this. Now look! You're sitting in jail facing involuntary manslaughter charges! Why couldn't you just listen to me?"

As angry as David's words made me I began to wish I had listened to him. *What the fuck was I thinking? How did I end up here? And, how would I get out of this? Fuck! What if I don't get out of this? What if I'm found guilty?* For the first time since C.J. shot his self I began to fully understand the predicament that I was in.

"I should have listened to you. I wish I had listened to you, but I didn't and now I'm in trouble. Please call Jack and get me out of here! They're about to move me to another jail. Tell Jack that I will be in San Francisco Jail #8. Please hurry!"

Nikko Allesandro was standing near a window when I entered the small gray room. His back was turned towards me and the first thing I noticed was his jet black hair. He was wearing a blue, pin-striped shirt and black dress pants. My eyes continued to scan his body until they reached his black dress shoes; they had a shine to them and without even seeing his face I imagined him to be a perfectionist. His jacket had been carefully placed on the back of a chair and his briefcase had been placed on top of the small metal table.

Nikko turned around and I noticed his piercing brown eyes. As he walked toward me he extended his arm and we shook hands.

"Hello! Tina Westbrook?"

"Yes, and you are?"

Nikko smiled and although he had a brilliant white smile, I noticed that one of his teeth was a bit crooked. I found that somehow charming. It gave him character; not that he needed character. Nikko Allesandro was an extremely attractive man.

"I'm Nikko Allesandro and I've been hired to represent you."

"Oh? And who hired you?"

Nikko smiled again. "I received a phone call this morning from Jack Gable, out of Birmingham. He requested that I come out here and see if I might be able to help you."

"Can you get me out of here? That would be a tremendous help!"

Nikko laughed and then motioned for me to sit down. "Your bail is being arranged; with any luck we will have you out of here before the day is over. You know you've been charged with involuntary manslaughter, right? Do you understand what that charge means?"

"I understand what that charge means, but I don't understand why I've been charged with it."

Nikko opened his briefcase and removed a legal pad and an ink pen. "Ms. Westbrook, currently in California there is an assisted suicide debate taking place. There are those that believe it should remain a crime, and then there are others that believe people have the right to die; if assistance is needed to make that possible, then so be it."

"I don't know how my situation has anything to do with a debate over assisted suicide. I didn't assist in anything."

Nikko began to tap his ink pen on the metal table. "Involuntary manslaughter or criminally negligent manslaughter occurs when death results from a high degree of negligence or recklessness. If an act is malum prohibitum it is not manslaughter unless the person who committed it could have forseen that death would be a direct result of the act."

I slightly smiled at Nikko and then the words just came out of my mouth, "Um, do you think you could say that again? Maybe this time you could use a language that I just might understand?"

"Ms. Westbrook, in the state of California you can be charged with involuntary manslaughter when the findings of the circumstances would lead a reasonable investigator to believe that it was you that were the one responsible for the death."

"Okay and Detective Tony Richter believes that I am responsible for C.J.'s death. So I get charged."

Nikko appeared to be pleased with his self. "Yes! Now you got it! It doesn't matter what you believe, it doesn't matter what I believe, what matters is what Detective Richter believes!"

"So, I get arrested for a crime that I didn't commit."

"Well, that's what's debatable. Were you negligent or reckless? Here's the good news - the charge of involuntary manslaughter is basically for clueless defendants. To sum it up, you have been charged because you should have known better."

My elbows were propped up on the metal table, fists below my chin, and I moved my hands to the side of my face. "This is all very confusing."

Nikko stood up and began pacing the floor. "Ms. Westbrook, involuntary manslaughter carries a two to four year prison sentence if convicted."

"What?! Are you telling me that I'm facing two to four years in prison for something that I didn't do? You know,

Richter is behaving as if I furnished the gun, or placed the gun in C.J.'s hands. I didn't do anything!"

"Again, you have to remember what the charge means. Is it a reasonable assumption that you could have forseen that a death would occur if you failed to take action?"

I just sat there. I couldn't say anything. The thought that I could somehow not only be responsible for C.J.'s death, but be convicted of involuntary manslaughter made me sick to my stomach.

"Ms. Westbrook, I know this doesn't sound good, but in reality, you're in a very good position right now. Assisted suicide is punishable as a second degree of manslaughter. Malice may be found if gross negligence amounts to wilful or depraved indifference to human life. In such a case, the wrong doer may be guilty of second degree murder."

"And, that's good, because?"

Nikko smiled and then gave me a small bit of hope. "It's good because they didn't charge you with second degree murder. They could have done that, and then the jury could have convicted you on a lesser charge, such as involuntary manslaughter. But they charged you with involuntary manslaughter, and California rarely convicts anyone of that. California's standard jury instruction for involuntary manslaughter states that criminal negligence involves more than ordinary carelessness, inattention or mistake in judgement. Key words here; More than! Were you careless? Perhaps; did you make a mistake in judgement? Perhaps, but was it more than ordinary? I don't think so."

Nikko seemed rather confident and it most certainly put me at ease. "So, they set a trial and then the prosecution has to prove that I was more than ordinarily careless?"

"Yes! However, I don't believe this will ever go to trial. Our first order of business is to get you out of here. In the meantime, I will pay a visit to the D.A.'s office and see if we can't just get the charges dropped. But, if they won't drop the charges, would you be willing to take a plea?"

I thought my eyes may pop out of my head when those words came out of Nikko's mouth. "Take a plea? Why would I do that? You just said yourself that California rarely convicts on involuntary manslaughter!"

"You're right, I did say that, but I never said never. If the prosecution refuses to drop the charges then we either take our chance in court, or you may plead guilty. If you were to plead guilty you would more than likely walk away with probation."

"There's no way in hell I'm going to plead guilty. I didn't do anything wrong. Did I? I mean, maybe I have this all wrong. Is it my fault that C.J.'s dead? Was I negligent, reckless or careless?"

Nikko placed his legal pad in his briefcase and closed it. "Well, that's for a jury to decide, if it comes to that. I'm heading over to the courthouse. Once you're released on bail where will you be?"

"I'm going back to Alabama."

"No, Tina, you're not. Once bail is posted you won't be allowed to leave the state of California unless a judge grants permission."

"So what am I suppose to do? How long before we can see a judge?"

Nikko started to put his jacket on and looked at me. "Let's see if we can get the charges dropped first. If not, then we'll see what we can do. Where will you be?"

"I've been staying at the Fisherman's Wharf Marriott, but I was expected to check out tomorrow."

"Okay, I will have my secretary call the hotel and make sure that your room remains as it is."

Nikko slid a few business cards across the table and extended his arm so that we could shake hands. "I will be in touch and if you have any questions or need anything, please call me."

Feeling the hot water pulsate against my body caused me to close my eyes and think of C.J. I could see his face clearly and envisioned his hand running through his hair. My eyes began to fill with tears and within moments I found myself crying uncontrollably. Flashbacks of the short amount of time we had spent together filled my head and I desperately wanted to turn back the hands of time. His voice was inescapable and his words echoed in my brain.

"I do feel safe. I still feel as if I can tell you anything. That's why I'm going to tell you this: You're lying! That's not what you were thinking. I can read you like a book and right now you're trying to figure out how to change the subject."

Recalling that conversation with C.J. unexpectedly made me laugh out loud. C.J. had spent year's people watching and he was a very quick study. He had been right. He could read me like a book. From the moment I met him I was captivated by him. I found him incredibly sexy and if truth be known I had felt that long before meeting him in person. His letters had stirred something within me; still unable to explain what that something was, but I knew then and I know now that those letters had forever changed me.

"Tina, come with me! My son just arrived and I want to introduce the two of you!"

My eyes flew open and I wished those words had not interrupted my train of concentration. As I turned off the water and reached for a towel I began to wonder if I would ever be capable of remembering C.J. and our time together without Chuck invading my thought process.

I would imagine that most people finding themselves in a situation such as mine may have blamed C.J. for putting them there, but I didn't blame him at all; I blamed Chuck. Chuck may resemble his father in appearance, but as far as I could see that was the only similarity between the two. C.J. was a kind, loving man with a conscience and those were qualities that I had yet to see Chuck exhibit.

After wrapping myself in a towel I turned out all the lights and stretched out across the bed.

Door Leading to Dungeon.

Photo by: Janice Fife

Robert Stroud's Cell.

Photo by: Janice Fife

Tina Westbrook & John Catelli, aka Mr. Alcatraz.

Photo by: Janice Fife

Original Alcatraz Fire Truck.

Photo by: Tina Westbrook

Capone,Alphonse #85

True Name: Capone,Alphonse,Gabriel
Aliases: Brown,Al
Costa,A
Capone,Scarface
Brown,Alphonse
Capone,Al
Capone,Alphonsus

Missing from Alcatraz for 40 years.

Escaped, 12-16-37, believed to have drowned
COLE, Theodore 258-AZ

Offense: Kidnapping
Sentence: 50 years
Sentence began: 5-20-35
Minimum date: 12-14-68
Maximum date: 5-19-85
Received, 10-26-35 from USP, LEAVENWORTH.

Missing from Alcatraz for 40 years.

Inside Guards Apartment.

Photo by: Tina Westbrook

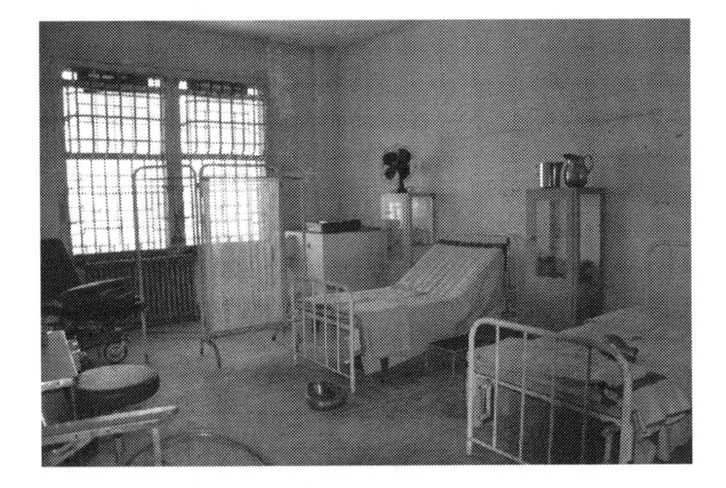

Alcatraz Hospital Ward.

Photo by: Janice Fife

Inside Alcatraz Dungeon.

Photo by: Tina Westbrook

Three

The ringing of the telephone woke me from my sleep and as I reached my arm out to grab it I noticed the time; 9am.

"Hello?"

"Rise and shine sweetheart! It's a beautiful day in the city! I was thinking we could take in some more sights today!"

I couldn't speak and my hand began to tremble. I sat up in bed and looked back at the clock. "What day is it?"

C.J. laughed, "What did you do last night? Can't even remember what day it is?"

My mind was racing and I grabbed the television remote control. "Seriously C.J., what day is it?"

"Are you okay? It's Thursday, June twenty first. I told you yesterday that I would be in touch. What's going on with you?"

Tears began to run down my face from sheer relief. "Oh my God…you wouldn't believe the dream I had last night. It was so…real."

"Well, get your butt out of bed and I'll pick you up in an hour. You can tell me all about it over breakfast, yes?"

"That sounds good. I'll meet you in the lobby!"

I exited the elevator and my eyes immediately caught a glimpse of C.J. standing near the hotel entrance. He was chatting away with a man and woman and all of them were smiling. Rather than walking right over to him I just stood there, watching him. To see him, really see him, alive and seemingly well, brought an unexplainable sense of peace and joy to my soul. I wanted to freeze that moment in time.

C.J. looked over and spotted me standing there. He smiled broadly and waved me over. As I approached him he reached out his hand and I felt the warmth as our fingers intertwined. The couple he had been speaking with walked out the door and C.J. kissed me on my forehead.

"I'm starving! Are you up for some breakfast?"

I wasn't really hungry, but I didn't care what we did or where we went. I felt as if I were having an out of body experience. The dream had been so realistic and it suddenly occurred to me that maybe *this* was a dream. We left the hotel and began walking in the direction of Alcatraz landing.

"So, tell me about your dream last night."

"It was awful…more like a nightmare. But, it seemed so real. I think my subconscious is fucking with me."

C.J. laughed, "It couldn't have been that bad…was it?"

"I dreamt you died and Chuck blamed me for it. Then I was arrested. It was terrible."

"It sounds to me like you're worried about something."

I stopped walking and C.J. turned to face me. "I am worried C.J. I'm worried about you. I'm worried whether or not you're okay. I'm worried that you may be...or may have been..."

C.J. interrupted me, "You're worried I'm going to kill myself? Is that what you're worried about?"

"Yes, I don't know what I would do if that happened. You can't do that to me. I would feel responsible if something happened to you."

"Why would you feel responsible if something happened to me?"

"Because, I would feel like I should have done something to prevent it. I know you say you're okay, but how can I be sure?"

C.J. smiled and with his hand still in mine began walking again. "You can only be responsible for your own actions. You can't take responsibility for what someone else may do. That's too much for anyone to worry with, but to set your mind at ease, I'm fine. I'm not going to lie to you; I thought about it. I've even planned for it. But, after leaving Alcatraz yesterday, and seeing my children, I knew I couldn't do it. So, it looks like you're going to just have to put up with me for a while longer."

I squeezed C.J.'s hand a little tighter and leaned my head on his arm. "So, maybe going back to Alcatraz wasn't such a bad thing after all?"

"You know Tina I usually avoid even looking in the direction of Alcatraz. But, when we got off the boat yesterday and I saw the hundreds of people waiting to get over there I realized, for the first time, the interest people have in that place. For me, it was just a part of my life, special yes, but just a small part. I have avoided Alcatraz all these years because of the memories of that last day. What I now realize is that one day doesn't define five years. I was one of the lucky few to experience Alcatraz in a way that most people can't even imagine. In fact, as we were leaving the island yesterday, I was approached by a staff member and invited to come back to tour the prison. Of course, we would be permitted to tour the entire prison, including area's that are off limits to the general public. What do you say? Should we go?"

I was caught off guard by what C.J. was saying. It was one thing to go over there to say goodbye to Diana, but to go over there and actually spend time on the island was something all together different. I wondered if he was ready to come face to face with all those memories. "Are you sure you're up for that?"

"I gave this a lot of thought yesterday and I feel like I'm not only ready, but I feel like it's time for me to let go of my past."

We continued our walk and found a restaurant for breakfast. Sitting down across from each other I found myself inundated with questions. So many things I wanted to know about this man and hoping that the right moment would come along for me to ask. I knew he would answer any question that I could conjure up, but asking them would take time. When delving into an individual's life it only seems right to tread lightly. I tried to put myself in his position; could I be so open about my life? It's very difficult to discuss intimate moments…to share those tiny details that we prefer to keep hidden. And, what gave me the right to ask? Yet, he had shared so much already. I couldn't grasp why I had the desire to know so much about him. I had never felt this way before.

Standing at the Alcatraz ticket booth I quietly watched as employee's greeted C.J. I don't think C.J. was prepared for the welcome that he received, but I'm not sure one can prepare for something like that. I knew his personal history with Alcatraz was special, but even I couldn't have imagined the warmth that was bestowed upon him. Watching it play out could only be compared to being in the midst of a celebrity and everyone trying to get to him. I watched as one young lady approached and asked him to sign the VIP book. We were whisked away to a private holding area where we would be given priority boarding on the next ferry. While we waited C.J. graciously posed for photos with Alcatraz employees.

Once the ferry arrived we were the first to board and we went to the top level. I'm not quite sure how it happened, but tourists had surrounded us and were asking all kinds of questions. I wondered if perhaps employees had pointed C.J. out to them as they waited in line to board.

I attempted to photograph Alcatraz Island and would look over at C.J. periodically, just to make sure he was doing okay. I thought about the last time I attempted to photograph Alcatraz. It had been extremely cold that day and there was a light mist. I shot those photographs with a Minolta 35mm film camera and I was thankful to be shooting with a Nikon SLR this time. I had worried whether or not any of those photographs would turn out and it was a good feeling to shoot and have the ability to look at the screen and instantly know if I had a good shot or not. I found myself thinking back to the day that digital camera's first came out. I was convinced it was a fad and it wasn't one that I was going to jump on board with; that now made me laugh.

I slightly leaned over the edge of the ferry, aiming my camera directly at the island when I felt a hand on my back. It startled me and I almost dropped my camera into the bay.

"I'm sorry! I didn't mean to catch you off guard!"

I turned around to find C.J. standing next to me, "I see you've broken away from all your admirers!"

"This is simply amazing. I guess I knew Alcatraz was a big deal, but I never imagined the interest people would have in my story."

I smiled at C.J., "You know, Alcatraz is part of American History. People are fascinated with the stories that came from this island. And, to meet someone that lived it? You may not get it, but I do."

C.J. wrapped his arms around my waist and pulled me closer to him. We were approaching the island and I could feel the warmth of his breath on my neck. We embraced for several minutes, oblivious that anyone else was around. In a whisper I asked him if he was okay.

C.J. pulled away, hands still on my waist and offered a slight smile, "I'm okay and I'm happy you're here with me. I don't think I could have come here without you."

Exiting the ferry we were once again surrounded by members of the Alcatraz staff. We would be spending the next three hours with a gentleman who was affectionately referred to as Big Hal. It only took a moment to understand how he got his name. He was extremely tall, towering over C.J. and myself. I briefly wondered if he was that tall, or if we were that short. Later that day we would be introduced to another member of Alcatraz security that was even taller than Big Hal. It was during that time that I really began to wonder.

The first stop on our three hour tour was at the old fire truck. It was roped off and people were not allowed to touch it. As I walked around the truck, photographing it from every imaginable angle, I smiled as I listened to C.J. explain to Big Hal how that fire truck used to be his play toy on the island.

On several occasions, after partaking heavily in alcohol, C.J. would jump in that truck and drive it around the island, with lights flashing nonetheless. Big Hal was quite amused and pulled several members of security over so that he could repeat the story to them. Before I knew it, Big Hal pointed to the fire truck and told C.J. to jump on. I absolutely could not believe what I was hearing and with C.J. smiling like a kid on Christmas morning I captured every moment with my trusty Nikon. Of course, this drew attention from the tourists that were nearby and once again we were bombarded with questions and had to repeat the story several more times.

I intently watched and listened to C.J., once again finding myself drawn to this man; searching for words to describe what I was feeling proved impossible. Many would simply explain it as attraction, but it was so much more than that. I felt love for him, yet the word love doesn't accurately describe the bond that I felt existed between the two of us. Days later, while sitting in front of my computer uploading nearly two thousand photographs, I would fully understand how I felt in that moment.

C.J. approached me and took me by the hand, "We're going to see the apartments where the guards and their families lived."

Oh Holy Cow! I couldn't believe the access that we were given and the adrenaline shot through my body. Big Hal advised us to be very careful and pointed to bricks that had fallen from the building.

Once inside C.J. and Big Hal continued their conversation and looking back now I wish I had lingered behind with them, but the photographer inside me took over and I began to photograph every little detail of the apartment that we were now standing in. From the peeling paint to the kitchen cupboards, there wasn't an inch that I didn't photograph.

If I had any regrets from our day spent at Alcatraz it would be that I missed some of C.J.'s stories. I now wish I had put down that camera and allowed his stories to take me back to a different time.

I turned the corner, leaving C.J. and Big Hal in another room and what I saw temporarily stopped me in my tracks. At first my mouth opened, but the words wouldn't come out. I shot a couple frames of what I was seeing and then I called for C.J. When he walked into the room I just pointed at what I found.

"Are you kidding me? Did you just do that?" C.J. thought I was pulling a prank on him.

"No! I didn't do that! I turned the corner and here it is!"

Big Hal walked into the room and saw what we were looking at. "Hah! You're going to find several things around the island that are going to surprise you!"

C.J. walked a bit closer and then looked up at Big Hal, "So, how did this get here?"

"Oh, no idea...Perhaps it was done by a family member that toured the island with us? Perhaps it's always been there."

The look on C.J.'s face made it impossible to hide what he was feeling. As he stood in front of that broken window I too had visions of Jake and Sandra. The cracked, dusty window pane seemed to be questioning what had taken him so long. Written in the dust was their last name.

Our next stop was Alcatraz Gardens, a photographers dream. Several volunteers were there tending the gardens and Big Hal introduced us to everyone. Once again, a crowd gathered around C.J. and I quietly took to photographing the large variety of plants. As I zoomed in on them it was apparent that they were well cared for. A woman wearing a volunteer shirt approached me and began to tell me how exciting it was to meet C.J. She had not been a volunteer long and this was the first time she ever met someone that had a direct connection to the prison.

"I think it's really great how all of you care for the grounds here. It's absolutely breathtaking!"

Polly smiled and began to explain how the gardens were first developed, then neglected, and now tended to again. "Most people that are fascinated with Alcatraz direct that fascination toward the prison and the inmates, but Alcatraz is so much more than that. The island was first inhabited in the mid 1800's; it was used as an army fortress. In 1861 it became a military prison and during that time the military began importing soil over from the Presidio and Angel Island. They were attempting to make the island more livable."

"Did they also begin planting then?"

"No, not immediately...it was in 1865 that they began to plant Victorian-style gardens near the citadel on the summit."

"That's really very interesting. I have studied the prison quite extensively, but I'm afraid to say that I never really paid much attention to the grounds, or how they came to be."

Polly smiled, "That's okay...you're not alone. Unless one has a passion for horticulture, they tend to overlook the true beauty of the island."

"So when did gardens become such an integral part of the island?"

"Oh, it wasn't until the 1920's. That's when the military and the California Spring Blossom and Wildflower Association joined forces in an island wide beautification project. Military prisoners planted hundreds of trees and shrubs. I forget how many pounds of seeds they planted, but it was several. Would you believe that plants from the military gardens are still in place today?"

"That is truly amazing; this island has seen so much, and the gardens were neglected for quite some time, weren't they?"

"Yes, but not the entire time. In 1933 Alcatraz became a Federal Prison and the Secretary to the Warden began caring for the gardens. At that time there were rose gardens, terraces and even a greenhouse. The secretary then convinced the warden to allow prisoners to garden. One prisoner, Elliott Michener tended the gardens for nine years. Between 1941 and 1950 he spent nearly every day of those nine years planting, ordering seeds and bulbs, building a tool shed and a greenhouse. He was quoted as saying that the experience provided him a *'lasting interest in creativity.'* The prison closed in 1963 and the gardens were abandoned."

"What happened when the island became part of the Golden Gate National Recreation Area?"

"Well, that happened in 1972, but the gardens were over-grown and some plants were unable to survive without maintenance and irrigation. On the other hand, many others spread across the island."

"So how did we get where we are today?"

"In 2003 the Garden Conservancy, Golden Gate National Parks Conservancy, and National Park Service collaborated to restore the gardens. Forty years passed before the gardens were cared for again, but with love they have thrived!"

C.J. had approached and listened as Polly and I wrapped up our conversation. Once finished I walked over to where he was standing.

"Wow that was really interesting! Until we came here today I had no idea that people volunteered their time to maintaining this island the way they do."

"I'm telling you C.J., people truly love this place. They take pride in caring for it."

"Yeah, it just reminds me of how much I loved being here. I guess that's why it was so hard to come back. My last memory of Alcatraz Island was of the destruction caused by the Indians. There was so much destruction and sadness, but I'm glad I came back. To see people caring for the island and loving it does a heart good. So, you ready? We're going to walk over to the bird sanctuary."

"I'm good to go!"

I said goodbye to Polly and C.J. and I joined Big Hal.

"Oh my God…I can't believe this is now the bird sanctuary." We were standing next to a six foot tall fence and birds were flying in all directions. C.J. stood there, staring at the rubble that had been left behind. "Do you know where we are?"

Without thinking I replied, "The bird sanctuary?"

C.J. smiled and placed his arm around me, "Yes smart ass, we're at the bird sanctuary, but this used to be where Jake and Sandra lived."

It had not even occurred to me to ask where their house had been located. C.J. began explaining how the house had been laid out, where the fireplace was and pointed to the area where the front door had once stood. "That's where I busted my ass when Diana left the front door open and it was pouring outside."

My thoughts immediately returned to the letter he wrote regarding that incident.

It was our third night on the island and we were beginning to become a bit stir crazy. It was raining very hard and extremely cold outside. Diana heard a noise around 11:30pm and decided that I should go investigate. I got out of bed and made my rounds throughout the house. Needless to say, I found nothing. After returning to the bedroom Diana informed me that the noise, she believed, was coming from outside the house, and I should go investigate. I was not willing to go outside in the cold and rain only to discover that it was a tree limb brushing against the house or perhaps a bird.

Now, I love my wife; I loved her then and I love her now. However, at that moment I saw a person that I didn't know. Diana jumped out of bed, grabbed her bathrobe, shoved her feet in her slippers, grabbed a flashlight and said "Fine. I guess I'll be the man tonight." Well, do whatever you want to do. I smugly returned to the warm bed that I was so rudely asked to leave and then guilt set in. What was I doing? What if someone was out there? What if something happened to her? So, I jumped back out of bed and headed toward the door, which Diana had left wide open. The rain was coming down sideways and the floor was soaked. I felt myself losing my balance, but there was nothing I could do to stop the fall. Bam, straight down on my back. As I attempted to get back up Diana entered the house. She was soaked to the bone, took one look at me, and said "Don't bother coming now!"

I didn't photograph the bird sanctuary; it didn't occur to me to do so at the time. Instead, I stood there quietly with C.J. I couldn't begin to imagine the thoughts that were going through his head right then. It felt as if we were standing at a sacred spot. I imagine memories were flooding his brain. I began to search my mental database and pulled out another letter that he had written me about his time on the island.

It was 6pm that evening as I approached the docks again. I boarded a ferry and with much anticipation I was on my way to Alcatraz. As the ferry moved closer to the island I began to imagine how Diana would react as she realized that I had forgone my original Christmas plans and traditions to be with her.

I arrived at Alcatraz Island and as I exited the ferry I spotted Jake. We shook hands and made our way to his house.

Instead of walking directly in, we knocked on the door and inside the house Sandra instructed Diana to answer the door.

The door swung open and Diana screamed with delight. She threw her arms around me and kissed me as if she hadn't seen me in years.

"I'll give you a penny for your thoughts."

"Oh, I was just thinking about a letter you wrote me a while back."

C.J. smiled, "It wouldn't be the one where I busted my ass would it?"

"Oh, no, I thought of that one earlier!"

C.J. and I both laughed and Big Hal asked if we were ready to go inside Alcatraz.

Once inside the prison our first stop was at Warden Johnston's office. Immediately upon entering C.J. stopped in front of a framed photograph hanging on the wall. It was a photo of Jake and two other guards on duty. This was the first time I had seen a photograph of Jake and I was surprised to find he looked just as I imagined him. I slightly moved back and took a photo, unbeknownst to C.J., of him standing in front of that photo.

This time of year often finds me thinking of Jake. He was such a wonderful man and I miss him terribly. Jake was the not the father in law that most young men hate to end up with. Jake was warm and friendly, and he always knew what to do and what to say; even when I didn't. I loved my own father, and I miss him as much as I miss Jake, but Jake seemed to understand me; more than anyone else. He once told me that when he looked at me he saw himself all too often. Perhaps he took pity on me! If that were the case he never let it be known.

As we wandered around Warden Johnston's office I thought it was rather ironic that Jake would be the last one standing on this Island. Long after Warden Johnston was gone, long after the prison had closed down and all the prisoners had left, Jake was still here.

Jake had served as a guard on Alcatraz Island from 1941 to 1963 and after the prison closed down he stayed on, hired by the GSA, as caretaker of the property. He had been there during the Indian invasions and didn't leave until 1971. 30 years spent on Alcatraz Island.

I vaguely remember the drive back home. I vaguely remember the days that followed that fateful night. I do, however, remember the moment that Diana and I told our children that Nana and Papa were gone. Diana tried, but couldn't hold the tears at bay. The children were so young and I vividly remember thinking how they were cheated. Diana and I both worried that in time they would forget their grandparents. It was shortly after the funeral when Diana and I decided that we would continue to celebrate Jake and Sandra's birthdays. We also vowed that every year, on the date of the accident, that we would all visit them at the cemetery. Our children would never forget Jake and Sandra. We would never let them.

Big Hal walked over to me and placed his hand on my shoulder, "Do you believe Alcatraz is haunted?"

I smiled, wondering if he thought it was. "I don't know…I saw an episode of Ghost Hunters recently that was filmed here and the ending really blew my mind. What do you think?"

"Oh, I don't believe in ghosts, but there are a lot of people here that do. I've heard all the stories, but I've never witnessed anything. Some say down in the shower area they can still hear Al Capone playing the banjo. You know, that's something I wouldn't mind hearing!"

Both Big Hal and I laughed, "You know Hal, maybe that's why you don't ever see anything or hear them. I think you have to be a believer first. Or, at least have an open mind. Give that some thought and maybe you'll get a visit from Al himself!"

"Now that I would like to see; I have studied and read everything ever written about Al Capone."

"Really? You know, I was born in Chicago and raised in Cicero. I guess you know all about that town, huh?"

"Yes I do!"

"It was pretty much run by the mafia. In fact, the elementary school I attended was built by money provided by Al Capone. He wasn't all bad. The way I understand it, anytime he had someone killed he supported the wife and family of his victim afterwards. Nice guy, huh?"

Hal and I were having a good time talking about ghosts, the mafia and Al Capone, and when we reached Capone's cell I was surprised to find the sign that used to hang above it was no longer there.

"Hey...where's the sign that used to hang up there? You know...it said *Al Capone's Cell.*"

"Oh, they took it down; too many people gathering in one spot at the same time. I managed to tape that small piece of paper there. I felt like we needed to mark the cell somehow."

"Way to go Hal!"

I looked around to find C.J., but didn't see him anywhere. "Hey, where did C.J. go?"

"Oh...he's right over there. I'm keeping an eye on him. It looks like some more staffers are asking questions. Let's grab him and go to the hospital."

The hospital and the clinic makes you wonder if there was ever a time when it appeared updated. With all of today's technology it strikes one as if this could have never been a good place to get sick.

The hospital ward is most famous for housing Robert Stroud, the Birdman, for eleven of the seventeen years he spent at Alcatraz. He arrived at Alcatraz in 1942 and remained in isolation. Due to his failing health he was moved to the hospital ward in 1948 and remained there until 1959. It was in 1959 that he was transferred to the Federal Penitentiary in Springfield, Missouri.

"Hey Hal...I hear that Stroud's cell is haunted."

"Yep...that's what they say. You know, everyone thinks Stroud was crazy, but I don't believe that."

I laughed, "I don't either. I think he was just smarter than everyone else! I mean, look at this place! It's what...

nine or ten times larger than a standard cell? He had plenty of room - no one to bother him. Yeah, he knew what he was doing!"

After photographing the entire hospital ward, along with Stroud's cell, we headed down to the shower area and Big Hal pointed out the spot where Al Capone had been stabbed by another inmate. We also visited the dining hall, the recreation yard, and the control room.

Big Hal showed us a long, narrow panel on the wall and to our surprise he unlocked it, revealing the lever used to open and close all cell doors. From that lever a guard could operate the cell blocks without going near them. I managed to get in a couple of shots of that. But, the big surprise was still ahead.

Big Hal walked us to the front of cell block A, which is off limits to tourists. There we discovered a staircase that led down to a large steel door. One literally has to bend over to keep from knocking their head off.

We were given hard hats to wear and informed that we could only stay down there for a few minutes, due to the asbestos in the air. Behind the steel door were corridors and stone archways. The smell can best be described as musty and moldy. It was here, in this underground hell hole, that the dungeons were tucked away.

Prisoners sent to the dungeons were chained to the walls and Big Hal shined his flashlight so that we were able to see the scratch marks imbedded in the concrete walls. "Prisoners would scratch the concrete with their nails," he explained.

They were stripped of their clothing and chained to the wall, in a standing position, from 6am to 6pm. They were given two cups of water and one slice of bread daily. On the third day they were given a solid meal. This was the most severe punishment for a prisoner, but not the only punishment.

Alcatraz had a single cell that was referred to as the "Strip Cell." The dark, steel encased cell had no toilet and no sink. There was only a hole in the floor. Inmates that were sent to the strip cell were given little food and no clothing. There was a standard set of cell bars with an expanded opening to pass food through, but after shutting the cell door a solid steel door would slam shut behind that, leaving the prisoner in total darkness. Inmates sent to the strip cell usually remained for one to two days.

Then there was the "Hole." The "Hole" was the place that prisoners regarded as inhumane and severe punishment. There were several of these cells and all were located on the bottom tier of the prison. Those sent to the "Hole" received bread and water, with a solid meal every third day. Inmates could spend up to nineteen days there and were left in complete silence and isolation. Men sent to the "Hole" often emerged from the darkness completely senseless and would end up in the prison's hospital ward. Some were void of any sanity while others suffered from arthritis and pneumonia after spending days and sometimes weeks on the cold cement floor with no clothing.

"I've read so much about inmates losing their sanity during their stay at Alcatraz."

"Warden Johnston didn't believe it was possible for an inmate to lose their sanity. He believed that mental illness was just an excuse to get out of work. He ran this prison with an iron fist. When Henry Young went on trial for the murder of another inmate; his accomplice in a failed escape attempt, Johnston was subpoenaed to testify about the prisons conditions and policies. In addition to calling on Johnston they also had several inmates testify. They told of being locked in the dungeons and beaten by guards. It's often been said that the guards were as hardened as the inmates by this place. At the end of the trial the jury sympathized with Young and he was convicted of manslaughter, which only added a few extra years to his sentence."

The three of us walked outside the prison and wandered over to Warden Johnston's house. The words that C.J. had written me were flashing through my mind.

Sadly, they had burned down the doctor's house. It was complete and utter pandemonium and destruction. In addition to burning down the doctor's house, they torched the wardens beautiful home. I had been in this house several times and it was just beautiful! The house sat on top of a hill overlooking a 360 degree perimeter of the gorgeous San Francisco Bay.

C.J. had emailed me photographs of Warden Johnston's home that he had taken back in the late sixties and standing in front of it now saddened me. I had stood in this exact spot years before, even photographed it, but having never seen the house during its glory days I really had not been able to comprehend the destruction. That was no longer the case.

As the three of us walked over to the boarding dock C.J. glanced up at the United States Penitentiary sign. Although now faded, the words that the Indians had written in red paint were still visible. *Welcome Indians.* C.J. commented that he was surprised that it had never been removed. I momentarily thought about that and understood how it must sting for him to see it, but I also understood the importance of it still being there. The

Indian invasion of Alcatraz is part of history. To remove it would be altering history.

As Big Hal and C.J. resumed their conversation I thought about Richard Oakes. A photograph of Oakes, along with several other Indians, was on display inside the prison and C.J. had told Hal about meeting him during the second invasion.

"He seemed to be a genuine, nice guy. He was willing to die for what he believed in and I respected him for standing up for what he thought was right. Unfortunately, I'm not sure he realized how destructive his behavior was. He did a lot of good things, but trouble seemed to follow him everywhere he went. His step-daughter fell here on the island, and died from massive head injuries. Shortly after that, Oakes left Alcatraz and he was involved in a bar fight, hit with a pool cue, and spent nearly thirty days in a coma. Remarkably he survived, but in September 1972 he was shot to death by Michael Morgan. Morgan was a YMCA camp manager who had a reputation of being rough with Indian kids. Unfortunately for both Oakes and Morgan, he made the mistake of doing it in front of Oakes one day. An argument broke out and Morgan shot Oakes to death. Oakes was only thirty-one when he died. To add insult to injury all charges were eventually dropped against Morgan; they determined that Oakes had moved aggressively toward him."

The ferry that we planned on taking back to Fisherman's Wharf was pulling in and we thanked Big Hal for taking the time to show us around Alcatraz and for allowing us special access. He walked us over to the boarding station and once again we were allowed to board prior to everyone else that was waiting.

Hal asked C.J. if he would consider coming out to the Alcatraz Reunion and he gladly accepted. It was in that moment that I knew returning to Alcatraz was a good thing and I was, and still am, thankful that I was given the opportunity to be with C.J. on that day.

Four

Arriving back at Fisherman's Wharf C.J. and I concluded that it was margarita time. We walked along looking for a good place to have a few drinks and eat, finally deciding on Boudin Cafe. We opted for a table on the balcony and settled in.

"Okay, what was your favorite thing about visiting Alcatraz today?"

I smiled and let my heart do the talking, "Well, I loved every bit of it. The guard's apartments were special, especially after finding the name written in dust. The dungeons were fascinating. I never imagined, not in my wildest dreams, that we would be given access to that area of the prison. I thoroughly enjoyed talking to the volunteer's with Alcatraz Gardens, and Big Hal is someone that I will remember for the rest of my life! But, at the end of the day, my favorite thing about visiting Alcatraz was being there with you."

"Well then…I guess I can let you in on a little secret. I would have never gone back if you weren't with me. During Diana's memorial all I could think about was getting back on that ferry and getting off that island. But, now that we've gone, I'm glad I did. I saw Alcatraz in an entirely new light. I never wanted to go back because of the memories of how it all ended over there, but the entire island seems to have been given new life. Now I can let go of that last day and remember the five years I spent there. And, I have a new last day. One spent with someone I love dearly."

Our drinks arrived and we toasted Alcatraz Island. I couldn't take my eyes off C.J. and it amazed me how a place like Alcatraz could bring two people from across the country together.

"I almost dropped over dead when I heard you tell Big Hal that you had the cards on Capone and Cole and that you wanted to return them to Alcatraz."

"While we were walking around and looking at all the items preserved for all these years I decided the cards belonged there. They didn't belong to me and they should be in their rightful place."

"Well, I think that what you're doing is remarkable. Not many people would do that. Did you happen to notice Hal's eyes light up when you told him that you would also provide photo's from the wedding and the time you spent there?"

"Hah…I thought he may break out in a happy dance."

Our server approached the table and we placed our lunch orders; French Onion Soup for me and a Waldorf salad for C.J.

"I was thinking…after lunch what do you think about taking in some more sights? I'd love to show you everything."

Smiling at C.J., I once again said the first thing that came to mind; never thinking of how it may sound, "I'd love for you to show me everything!" Once the words came out of my mouth I realized what I said and judging by C.J.'s reaction, that's exactly how he interpreted it. He slightly lowered his head and even though he was wearing sun glasses I could see his eyebrows were raised. A smile came across his face, but not the usual smile. This was more of a seductive smile.

"Is that right?"

"You're such a flirt!"

"Me? You said it."

"Mmm Hmm...I said it, but you know what I meant!"

"I'm not sure about that...perhaps your subconscious is fucking with you again?"

C.J. leaned back in his chair and once again my imagination began to go places that it shouldn't have been going. I thought about the words I said to C.J. two days earlier. *Well done C.J.! You're right. That's not what I was thinking. I was thinking what might happen if neither one of us were married. I was thinking that you are perhaps the sexiest man I have ever met. Feel better now?* Of course I said those words without yet having the knowledge that Diana had passed away. Would I have said them had I known?

Our lunch arrived and we ordered another round of drinks. We sat on that balcony for two hours; drinking, eating and chatting up every topic that came to mind. The majority of our conversation dealt with the everyday, non-essential things that most people talk about - Then it turned to marriage. I can't recall who brought it up first, but I definitely remember what C.J. said.

"Everyone has this notion that I must have been the perfect husband. It's funny how people, looking in from the outside, can come to certain conclusions. They just assume things. Perception is reality."

"You must have been doing something right. Look how long your marriage lasted. Literally 'til death do us part."

"My marriage only lasted because I happened to marry a woman that refused to see what was going on. You know...don't ask, don't tell. In all our forty years she never asked me if I cheated on her. All the signs were there. Hell, at one point she practically caught me and when I arrived home not a word was spoken. I think she wanted me to feel guilty and she wasn't going to give me the satisfaction of knowing it upset her."

"Looking back on it now, if you could go back and change the things you did, the way you lived your life, would you?"

"I have a lot of regrets; you're asking me a difficult question. I did what I did because I wanted to. No one forced me. I lived my life as if I had the right to do whatever felt good at the moment. Would I change what I did? You're going to have to let me roll that question around for a little while."

I smiled, "Take your time!"

As we finished our lunch we discussed where to go next. We decided to make our first stop Coit Tower. I had never been there and C.J. explained the amazing views from the top. I didn't need to hear anything else. The entire city of San Francisco is one photo op after another and I was excited to shoot the city from a new perspective.

"The answer is no."

I turned to find C.J. standing behind me, "What?"

"You asked me if I would change the way I lived my life and the answer is no. I feel bad about the way I lived my life at times, but would I change it? Absolutely not - my experiences are what made me who I am today. At times I wish I had the strength to walk away from certain things…I wish I had been that person, but I wasn't."

We were standing at the top of Coit Tower near a window and C.J. pointed, "You can see Lombard! How cool is that?"

I focused my camera and took several shots of the famous street and when I turned back around I discovered that C.J. had walked over to the other side. I shot several frames of him photographing the city.

"I bet you never get tired of seeing this." This time C.J. turned around to find me standing there.

"You're right, I don't. I'm in love with this city, always have been. I've been photographing it for as long as I can remember."

"I can understand that. This city is alive. Very few cities have the ability to pull people in. The moment you arrive here adrenaline just shoots through your body. It's an exciting place."

"So, you can understand how one could find their selves getting into a little trouble here every now and again?"

"Hah, I don't know about that. There are some people in this world that look for trouble. There are others that avoid trouble at all costs, yet on occasion get caught up in it. And, there are those that attract trouble; whether they're looking for it or not. I think you're the latter."

"I attract trouble?"

"Yes, I do believe you do. It doesn't matter what you're doing, where you're at, if trouble is anywhere in the vicinity it's going to find you."

"Why do you think that is?"

"Because I think you thrive on it. I think you enjoy pushing the envelope. I think you get a thrill out of seeing just how much you can get away with. And, I think you have a huge ego. So, being extremely attractive, you get away with things that the ordinary person couldn't get away with. To make it even easier, you come across as the nicest man anyone could ever hope to meet."

"Damn, am I that easy to read?"

"Am I right?"

C.J. kissed me on my cheek, "I do believe I have met my match."

The attraction between C.J. and I was undeniable and flirting with each other seemed to come as second nature. To describe him accurately, completely, would prove to be a difficult task. To say he was handsome would truly be an understatement. He was blessed with movie star good looks; from the top of his head all the way down to his tan, muscular legs.

I studied every inch of his face and found myself unable to determine what his best feature was. It came down to his eyes and his smile. A woman could easily get lost looking in his eyes. His smile at times made me weak in the knees and I found the little laugh lines around his eyes incredibly sexy.

What fascinated me most was his ability to still come across as approachable. This, I determined, was how he managed to pull so many women in. People have a tendency to feel intimidated by an extremely good looking man, or woman for that matter, but C.J. never felt intimidating. His personality always shined through and people were drawn to him.

During my visit to San Francisco I watched as one woman after another practically swooned in his presence. I watched as he communicated with them. The way he would flash his smile, touch them on the hand, or move in closer to them. He had the art of seduction down to a science.

C.J. was a womanizer yet he knew how to work it without ever coming across as one. I appreciated the fact that it must have taken him years to develop his technique. This topic would be one that we would discuss in great detail later that night.

The drive to Sausalito didn't come without a quick stop along the way. The sun was beginning to set and we detoured to Baker Beach in an attempt to capture the perfect shot as the sunlight gently moved across the Golden Gate Bridge.

Baker Beach is a public beach on the peninsula of San Francisco; lying on the shore of the Pacific Ocean to the northwest of the city. Approximately half a mile long, beginning just south of the Golden Gate Bridge and extending southward toward the Seacliff peninsula, Baker Beach is considered a nude beach.

We exited the car and began walking toward the water's edge. The wind was softly blowing and I stopped momentarily to remove my high heels.

Several boats were in the water and a rowing team slowly passed by. Both C.J. and I began shooting the bridge, boats and anything else that we found interesting. At one point I turned to take a picture of C.J. only to find he was about to take a picture of me. We pushed the shutter at the same time and now we each have photos of the other with a camera in our face.

I photographed C.J. a lot during that trip. Rarely do I find an individual that I actually enjoy photographing. It would be easy to assume that I enjoyed photographing him because of his appearance, but that would most definitely be the wrong assumption. I wanted to remember every moment spent with him. I learned long ago that memories fade, but a photograph can take you back to a time and place. Through photography memories are brought back to life; little details, long forgotten, are instantaneously recalled. People are frozen in time.

"Are you cold?"

"I'm getting a bit chilly. My body can't accept the fact that it's only fifty nine degrees at the end of June."

"Hah...you're not in Alabama anymore!"

"Definitely not...it was ninety eight when I left home and well above one hundred with the heat index."

"Well, if you're done shooting let's get going. Maybe a drink will warm you up."

"I'm sure it couldn't hurt!"

Once back in the car C.J. turned the heat on low and I slowly felt my toes beginning to thaw.

"Are you hungry?"

"Actually, I am. What about you?"

"I'm starving. There's a place in Sausalito called Scoma's that I thought we could go to. The food is out of this world and they make a pretty damn good drink too!"

"That works for me."

Sausalito is just minutes from San Francisco, across the Golden Gate Bridge. With a Mediterranean flair, Sausalito is a waterfront community and known worldwide for its breathtaking views.

After parking the car C.J. and I casually strolled in the direction of Scoma's, taking a few photos along the way.

We entered the restaurant and were seated immediately. After placing our drink orders we glanced over the menu and made our dinner choices.

"Are Isabella and Chuck still in town?"

"Yes, Bella's been staying with me at the house and Chuck's been staying in Oakland."

"I knew Chuck was staying in Oakland, why is that?"

"He has an old college buddy that lives out there. Chuck's been slightly pissed at me since Diana died, that's the only reason he's staying there. How did you know he was staying in Oakland?"

"We were seated next to each other on the plane. He mentioned it during our chit chat."

"It's a small world, isn't it?"

"Yeah, you can say that again. You could have knocked me over with a feather when I realized that the guy I sat next to on a plane all day was your son."

"Well, he was as surprised to see you as you were to see him."

"Why has he been pissed off at you since Diana died?"

"Oh, he had a telephone conversation with Diana a few days before she died and she mentioned to him that I had been spending too much time on the computer. I didn't know about the conversation until Monday night, after he arrived. I thought it was rather odd that he would be bringing it up a year after the fact, and the night before the memorial service at that, but he did and we got into an argument about it. I'm glad he went to Oakland."

"I'm sorry. We don't have to talk about this."

"There's nothing to be sorry for; it's good that he speaks his mind. Both he and Bella were raised to think for their selves and whether I agree or disagree with their opinions, I respect them."

"So he's mad because Diana felt like you were on line too much? It seems strange for him to be upset about something like that for so long."

"He blames me for Diana's death. He thinks she was so stressed out that she had a heart attack. After the memorial service yesterday he came back to the house and he found something that set him off. We ended up having another argument and he stormed out. I'm proud of my kids for standing up for what they believe in, but in no way will I accept either one of them being disrespectful. Chuck was way out of line and he needs to apologize for his behavior."

"So you haven't spoken to him since then?"

"I called him on his cell phone three times last night but he never answered. He took something out of the house that he had no right to take. I left him three messages telling him he better get his ass back to the house and return what he took before today is over."

"What did he take?"

"It was something that belonged to Diana. I don't know why in the hell he thought he had a right to it, but it was something very personal and I want it back. He went into my home office and took it."

"I'm sure he will return it."

"If he knows what's good for him he will. I'm not too old to kick his ass."

Our drinks arrived and I thought it may be a good time to change the subject, "I can't believe I'm leaving tomorrow."

"I know, it feels like you just got here. What time do you need to be at the airport?"

"My flight leaves at eleven thirty, so probably by ten."

"I'd be more than happy to drive you out there."

"Oh, that's sweet, but not necessary. I purchased round trip shuttle tickets. There's no reason for you to fight that traffic."

"Well, if you change your mind just say so. It's not like I'm so busy that I can't drive you out there."

"I know, but I'm sure you want to spend time with Isabella. When does she head back home?"

"Saturday morning."

"Then you definitely don't need to spend tomorrow morning going back and forth to the airport."

"Have it your way, but if you change your mind..."

"I know, thanks C.J. Hey, you mentioned earlier that Diana practically caught you cheating one time. How did that happen?"

"Oh, it was rather amusing actually. I had been fooling around with this woman that worked in an office across the street from the dealership. We had been seeing each other for about six months and I had gotten into the habit of telling Diana that I was working late; trying to get caught up on paperwork, meeting with the accountant, or staying late because new cars were coming in. I didn't realize I had increased the number of lies I was telling on a weekly basis. Sometimes three or four times a week I would lie so I could go see Rebecca. Well, on this particular day Rebecca called me and wanted to get together that evening, so I called Diana and told her that I would be home late; the accountant was coming over after hours to go through the books. It seemed to go over fine, but then I made a tremendous mistake. As I was leaving the office I called Diana again, from my cell phone, and told her that he had just arrived and I didn't know what time I would be home. Little did I know that Diana had the calls coming into the house transferred to her cell phone. So, as I'm telling her the accountant just arrived, she's sitting in her car, directly across the street, watching me walk out of the dealership. It wasn't until I got in my car and began driving to Rebecca's did I know I was in trouble. My cell phone rang, I answered it, and all I heard was, *you lying son of a bitch. If you have any idea what's good for you you'll turn your fucking car around and head home.* I looked in my rearview mirror and saw Diana's car behind me. I think I momentarily lost my sanity because instead of turning the car around I gassed it and lost her."

"That has to be the funniest thing I have ever heard."

"It wasn't very funny at the time. I drove around for about an hour trying to decide what I should do. I ended up calling Rebecca and telling her that I wasn't going to be able to come over after all. Then I went home. I'll never forget the look on Diana's face. I had prepared myself for a heated argument, but then she never said a word about it. I think she figured I had been caught and it wouldn't happen again. Her lack of words was her attempt at making me feel guilty, but it didn't work. Instead of feeling guilty I was pissed off that she ruined my evening. Now here's the really funny thing about it: Had I been thinking and hadn't let her rattle me the way I did, I would have simply said, *what are you talking about? I'm going to get us a bite of dinner.* Then I would have pulled into a drive through restaurant and let her follow me back to the dealership."

"So now that you knew she was on to you, did you stop seeing Rebecca?"

"No, I just changed my routine. Rebecca worked until three thirty and instead of going to see her when I got off work, a few days per week I would take my lunch break later."

"Was that the only time you ever got caught?"

"Yeah...if Diana ever suspected me of fooling around she never said anything to me about it."

"When did that happen?"

"That was in the early nineties, ninety two I think. I ended it with Rebecca when she started talking about wanting me to leave my wife. Why would I do that?"

"Oh gosh C.J., I don't know. Maybe she thought you were unhappy in your marriage and she could be the one to make you want to change your ways."

"Hah, she was sadly mistaken."

Our dinner arrived and the conversation turned to how good everything was. We ordered another round of drinks and enjoyed the food and each other's company.

We left Scoma's a little past ten and as we drove back to the hotel we made a quick stop to grab a bottle of wine. Our plan was to go up to my room, kick back and continue our conversation.

As C.J. opened the wine I removed my shoes, grabbed a pair of shorts and a tee shirt, went into the restroom and changed clothes. When I came out C.J. was sitting in a chair next to the bed with two glasses of wine. The room was quiet and the only light burning was the one that I had turned on as we entered the room. I crawled across the bed, from one side to the other, lying down on my tummy and C.J. handed me a glass.

"Cheers darlin', today has been one of the best days of my life."

I smiled and raised my glass, "I'll drink to that."

"You have really nice legs, has anyone ever told you that?"

"Are you flirting with me?"

"I must be losing my touch. I've been flirting with you since you got here."

Laughing, I reached my hand out, placing it in C.J.'s and lightly kissed the top of his, "You are such a doll. You know I love you, right?"

"I do, and I love you too."

I found it extremely difficult to take my eyes off C.J. and the desire to pull him close to me was overwhelming. As he made small talk my mind began to wander. I attempted to pay attention to what he was saying, something about Sausalito; something else about Coit Tower, but all I could think about was feeling his body next to mine.

"So what do you think?"

"Huh? What do I think about what?"

"Have you heard a word I've been saying?"

C.J. was smiling and I knew he could read my mind, "I may have been a bit distracted. Could you say it again?"

"No, I can't say it again."

"I'm sorry, I'll pay better attention."

"Hah, I just bet you will."

"How old were you when you realized you could pretty much get any woman you wanted?"

"Oh, damn, that didn't happen until after I got married. I dated a lot of women before I met Diana, and all my relationships were pretty much centered around sex, but back then that wasn't unusual. Everyone was having sex with everyone. Sex just wasn't a big deal."

"So it wasn't until after you were married that you understood, knew, that women were attracted to you?"

"I knew I was a good looking kid; I heard that all the time. But, during my teen years I was involved in a relationship that I shouldn't have been involved in. That kind of messed me up. Thinking about it now, I realize that it was that relationship that resulted in inappropriate behavior for the rest of my life. Because boundaries hadn't been respected, I lost sight of the fact that we all have boundaries. I never respected those boundaries; whether they were what society deemed as appropriate or the boundaries of marriage. Somehow they didn't seem to apply to me. The only thing I had going for me was the innate ability to pass myself off as a good kid while living a life that most would deem below standard."

"How old were you when you became involved in that relationship?"

Running his hand through his hair C.J. took a sip of wine, "I was sixteen. It wasn't my first sexual experience, that happened when I was fourteen, but it was my first long term relationship and it lasted until I was eighteen. My father's brother Lou recently remarried and had decided to move back to San Francisco. He and Marcie purchased a house just a few blocks from ours. Anyway, I came home from school one day to find Marcie at the house. Their oven wasn't working and she was using ours. To this day I don't know where my mother was...perhaps out shopping, but I was in the kitchen with Marcie when she came up from behind me. She started kissing the back of my neck and telling me how good I looked. I just froze in my tracks. Part of me was thinking *what the fuck is she doing?* But then she ran her hands across my chest, down my stomach, and began tugging at the button on my jeans. When I turned around to face her she began to kiss me. The next thing I knew clothes were coming off and we had sex right there in the kitchen. I honestly thought it was a one-time thing and I felt really bad about it, but we began finding ways to get together. A lot of days after school I would go to their house, fuck Marcie and then go home. It ended when they moved back to Oakland."

"Did you ever tell anyone about it?"

"Hell no...when I found out they were moving back to Oakland I was relieved. There were many occasions that we were almost caught and I felt trapped. The last thing I wanted was my parents to find out I had been sleeping with my uncle's new wife. But that was a major turning point in my life. I began to see women as just sexual objects. I could fuck them and in my mind I didn't owe them anything. It wasn't until I met Diana that I actually felt emotions for a woman, but the damage had already been done. I wanted the beautiful wife at home, the kids, the house, but I still felt it was my right to have as many women as I wanted. In my mind they were simply satisfying whatever urge I happened to have at any given moment."

"I find that very interesting. It's as if you were programmed to live two separate lives."

"That's a good word to use – programmed. I couldn't make sense of what I was doing in my head and I thought at times that there must be something wrong with me.

How could I love someone as much as I loved Diana, yet do something over and over again that I knew would devastate her if she found out about it? Yet, as I was doing it I never felt guilty. I felt as if I were entitled."

"And so the womanizer was born…"

"I never thought of myself as a womanizer, but looking back on my life I most definitely was. If I feel bad about it I only feel bad because women viewed me as something I wasn't. I always came across as if I cared about the women I became involved with. I knew it would never be more than sex, but they thought differently. I wonder how many would have been so willing to jump in bed with me if I had said something like *you know, I'm just going to fuck you and then go home to my wife. I could care less how you feel. I don't want you for anything but sex.*"

"Hah, you may be surprised C.J. There are plenty of women who still would have jumped in bed with you. The real question is, after hearing you say that, would they have still jumped in bed with you and thought they would be the one to change your mind? Women all seem to do that. It doesn't matter how loud a man screams *I don't want a relationship,* women don't hear it."

"That's funny…I have often said that when it comes to men, women have selective hearing."

"They do and they also have a desire to fix men. You were the perfect candidate. If anyone needed fixing it were you."

"Have you ever been cheated on?"

"If I have I don't know it. My father cheated on my mother a lot; you remind me of him. I always thought my mother was weak for putting up with it. It's not the sex that would piss me off, I get that; it's the lack of honesty. I have always felt like the man I'm with owes me one thing…if you're going to cheat on me, or you want to cheat on me, than you owe me the truth. Don't do it behind my back and let me find out from someone else. If you're man enough to do it than you should be man enough to tell me."

"If Diana had ever said something like that to me I may have given more thought to my actions. I think that's the problem. It was easy to ignore how my actions could affect her. It was too easy to leave the house, knowing she would be there when I came home. I lived in two different worlds; the world inside our home and the world outside our home. Once I walked out the door I had another life."

"How many different women would you say you slept with during your marriage?"

"Oh my God, I have no idea. Diana and I were together for forty years. If I were going to guess, I would say a minimum of two different women a year, but when I say that even I can't believe it. Were there eighty or ninety...maybe one hundred? The numbers really began multiplying in the late eighties and throughout the nineties."

"What happened then?"

"I began using cocaine. That's when I really thought I could do whatever I wanted to do. I became addicted to it and didn't get clean until 2000. Coke nearly destroyed me, my family and my future. I did all but clean out the bank accounts. If I could have gotten my hands on my 401K I would have used that too."

"So after all the drug use in the sixties and seventies, you jumped right back in?"

"I'm not sure I ever really jumped out. I've been an addict for as long as I can remember. I began smoking pot when I was a teenager and until the year 2000 I was always high on one thing or the other."

"Diana had to have known, didn't she?"

"Diana knew that on occasion I would smoke a joint. She never knew about the LSD. A few years after we were married I stopped using it completely, but I didn't stop altering my mind with other drugs. I used a lot of speed and my pot smoking was daily, not occasionally. I drank a lot and then the eighties came along. Cocaine was the worst thing I ever touched and I regret ever getting involved with it. I was pretty much addicted after using it twice. I hid it from Diana for a few years, but then the money began disappearing. Not just money from my paycheck, but massive amounts of money from bank accounts. She threatened to leave me if I didn't get clean, so off to rehab I went. I'd do fine, get out of rehab and then go right back to the coke. I ended up in rehab six times. Diana was fed up and I came home one day to find all my belongings had been packed. She kicked me out of the house and refused to take my calls or see me. That was in 1999 and it was the second time during our marriage that we separated; the first being in 1990. Diana had confessed a brief affair to me that she had been having and we split for a couple of weeks. At any rate, I hit rock bottom in 2000. I had been seeing this twenty-something year old girl and we were driving to Napa Valley for the weekend. I was driving too fast and not paying attention. The car in front of me slammed on its breaks and I plowed right into it. I was all coked up and the impact knocked me out. When I woke up I was in the hospital; that's when they told me I was under arrest for possession. The hospital released me and I was taken to jail. I knew better than to call Diana so I telephoned an old friend of mine. After he posted my bail I had him drop me off at the house, mine and Diana's. She was furious, but she drove me back to rehab and I stayed there until my court date came up. I've been clean ever since."

"Damn C.J., so how long were you and Diana separated that time?"

"Nearly a year; I had pretty much given up on thinking we would ever get back together. A day didn't pass that I wondered if that would be the day I'd be served with divorce papers. She must have loved me, because even I would have bailed out after what I put her through."

"Did Chuck and Isabella know what was going on?"

"They knew we were separated, but they never knew why. Of course Chuck didn't care why, no matter what had happened he knew it was my fault. Chuck has always been closer to Diana than me. But Bella, that's a different story. She's a daddy's girl. I think the problem with Chuck is that he knew more of what was going on than I ever realized. There have been several occasions through the years that he made it perfectly clear that he didn't think I treated Diana as well as I could have."

"What do you think?"

"I think I treated Diana as well as I knew how. I could not have loved her more than I did. I provided a good life for her and our children. I wasn't a saint, far from it, but I loved them and their well being was always my first priority. Was I reckless? Most certainly, but when it came to the three of them there's nothing I wouldn't have done to protect them. I just couldn't see how my actions affected them. I didn't want to see."

"So things changed once the two of you were back together?"

"Things most definitely changed. For the first time in my adult life I was clean. There were days that just getting out of bed was a struggle and on more than one occasion I came close to using again, but somehow I made it through. I had inherited the dealerships after my father died and in 2001 I sold them. Diana and I spent the next five years just enjoying life. I wish I had sold those damn dealerships long before 2001. If I had known I would lose Diana so soon I would have."

"Did you stop cheating on her after you retired?"

"I'd love to say I did, but I'd be lying," C.J. poured both of us another glass of wine and continued talking, "Women was the one addiction I couldn't kick."

"I guess everyone has their vice."

"I think they do! Some people smoke, some people drink, shop, gamble…everyone seems to have something."

I found that rather funny, "Yeah and you just fuck!"

"What can I say? Make love, not war!"

"Spoken like a true child of the sixties."

C.J. leaned over and kissed me on my forehead, "I'm going to miss you."

"I'm going to miss you too, but I want you to know that I fully expect that I will continue receiving my letters from Mr. Alcatraz."

"Oh, you don't even have to worry about that. I think I get more out of writing them than you do from receiving them. I always feel like I've had a good therapy session after I write to you."

"That's nice to hear. I always feel like I've just read a chapter from a favorite book."

C.J. glanced around the room, "What time is it?"

I sat up and looked at the clock sitting on the nightstand on the other side of the bed, "It's almost one."

"I guess I better get going. You need to get some sleep you have a long day ahead of you tomorrow. Have you changed your mind about letting me take you to the airport?"

"No, I'll be fine. Spend the day with Isabella and your grandchildren. I bet they would love that!"

"Okay, but if you change your mind call me. I'm always just a phone call away."

C.J. stood up and placed his glass on the desk. I felt sadness sweeping over me and I wasn't sure I could say goodbye to him without tears.

I was sitting on the edge of the bed when he walked over and held out his hands. Placing my hands in his he pulled me up and then leaned down to kiss me.

Our lips met, slightly parted, and I felt the warmth of his tongue slowly circle mine. His hands were on my waist and as he pulled me closer the desire to become one with him was overwhelming.

As our kiss came to an end he nuzzled his face against my neck and then whispered into my ear, "I love you."

"I love you too."

Pulling away he smiled and as he turned to walk toward the door I felt the sting of the first tear as it rolled down my cheek.

As I slid into bed I attempted to adjust the pillows and felt something hard. My hand grabbed at it and once the small box was firmly in my hand I sat up in bed and turned the lamp on.

Once the little box was opened tears began flowing freely. Inside that box was a silver, heart shaped locket with the words "I love you" engraved on the back.

Five

The alarm went off at 6am, allowing me an ample amount of time to pack, get myself together and get to the airport. My five days in San Francisco had come to an end and as much as I hated to go, I knew I had to.

After making several attempts to contact C.J., I finally gave up and opted for leaving him a message on his cell phone. I thanked him for the locket and told him how surprised I was when I found it. I also told him how much it meant to me. I placed the handset back on its cradle, threw my purse on my shoulder and grabbed the handle of my rolling luggage.

Entering the lobby I spotted Katie behind the front desk. This was the first time I had seen her since arriving, "Hello Ms. Westbrook, checking out?"

"I'm afraid I am."

"I hope your stay was enjoyable."

"It was - most definitely was, thank you."

I handed my room keys to Katie and turned to leave. I had barely taken three steps when I heard Katie call for me, "Ms. Westbrook, you have a call."

I turned around and saw Katie holding the telephone out toward me.

"Hello?"

"Thank God, I caught you!"

"Hey! I tried to call you to say goodbye, but I kept getting your voicemail."

"I know, I'm sorry, I took Isabella and the kids to breakfast this morning. I need you to do me a favor."

"Sure, what's up?"

"I need you to go to Alcatraz Landing. Chuck will meet you there."

"C.J., I don't understand. Judging by the look on Chuck's face at the memorial service he's not my biggest fan. Why would he be meeting me at Alcatraz Landing?"

"Because I can't, I'm at least forty five minutes away and you'll miss your plane. I have Bella and the kids with me. Please go meet Chuck. I gave him your cell number in case I wasn't able to find you. He's already in the city and he said he would wait for you there."

"Okay, I'll go meet Chuck, but I really wish you would tell me what's going on."

"All this time that we're on the phone is wasted time. Hang up the phone and go to Alcatraz Landing. You have no idea what I've been through the last six hours."

"Okay, I'm going…I'll call you later."

"Good, okay, have a safe trip. I love you."

"I love you."

I handed the telephone back to Katie and asked if I could leave my luggage with her for a little while. I looked outside and saw my airport shuttle pulling in.

"Hey Katie, how often do the shuttles run?"

"I think they run about every thirty minutes or so."

I didn't think I could make it to Alcatraz Landing, meet up with Chuck and get back in time to catch a shuttle bus and still get to the airport on time. Just then my cell phone rang. I thanked Katie and told her I would be back shortly.

"Hello?"

"Tina, this is Chuck."

"Hi, your dad just called."

"Are you going to be able to meet me at Alcatraz Landing?"

"I just left the hotel and I'm on my way. Would you mind telling me what's going on?"

"Oh, as if he didn't?"

"No Chuck, he didn't. He said that he had Isabella and the kids with him."

"You have a lot of fucking nerve, you know that? I can't believe you came to my mother's memorial service."

"Why is that Chuck?"

"If it weren't for you she would still be alive."

I almost dropped the telephone and I was stunned by what Chuck was saying to me. *If it weren't for me Diana would still be alive?*

"How is it my fault that your mother died?"

"It was too much stress for her to take. As if my father hadn't put her through enough over the course of their marriage. This whole damn thing was just too much for her."

"Chuck, I'm really very sorry your mother died, but I still don't understand what I had to do with it."

"No? You don't understand? How would you take it if your husband of forty years told you that he was in love with another woman?"

My head began to spin and I felt as if I were being strangled. It was becoming harder for me to breathe and my legs felt as if they were going to give out from under me. I stopped walking and leaned against the side of a building.

"What's the matter Tina? Cat got your tongue?"

"I…I don't know what you're talking about."

"You've got ten minutes to get here. If you're not here I'm leaving and I'm taking this fucking box with me. My father can go to hell if he doesn't like it."

Box…What box? "Chuck, I'm on my way. I don't know anything about a box and I don't know anything about C.J. saying anything like that to Diana. I think you have this all wrong, no, I know you have this all wrong. You're obviously very upset, but I think that perhaps talking to your dad will clear this all up."

"What the fuck do you think I've been doing since Monday? Sitting on my ass? I have talked until I'm blue in the fucking face. He's a liar, he's a cheater and he's not the man I thought he was. He wants you to have this fucking box, than fine, it's yours. But if you have a shred of decency you won't take it. It doesn't belong to you. You don't have the right to it."

"This is the first time I've heard anything about a box. What's inside the box?"

"My mother's life is inside this box. He doesn't think my sister or I have a right to the contents, but you do? Tell me something, how the fuck does that happen? What entitles you to it?"

"I'm sure nothing entitles me to it, but there has to be a reason C.J. wants me to have it. Did he not tell you?"

"When he realized I took this fucking box he lost his fucking mind. Fine, he didn't want me to have it…it belongs to him, that's just fine. But when I called him to say I was bringing it back he wants me to bring it to you? No, he didn't tell me why. I thought you could at least give me that much."

"I would if I knew, but I swear to you, I'm completely clueless. I was on my way to the airport when he called me. I've been here for five days and this is the first I've heard about any box."

"Jesus Christ, give me a fucking break. You've spent five days with him and he didn't tell you? You want me to believe that he never mentioned this? You're just like him, you're a liar."

"No, he never mentioned it. The only thing I know is that the two of you had an argument and after you left the house he realized you had taken something that belonged to Diana and he wanted it back. That's all he told me."

"Yeah, he wanted it back so he could give it to you. Time's running out…five more minutes and I leave."

"I'll be there! Don't leave."

I heard a click and realized Chuck had hung up on me.

He blames me for Diana's death. He thinks she was so stressed out she had a heart attack. C.J.'s words were now echoing in my head.

I had five minutes to get to Alcatraz Landing or Chuck was going to leave and I needed to make sense of what both he and C.J. had said to me.

He had a telephone conversation with Diana a few days before she died and she mentioned to him that I had been spending too much time on the computer.

With the sun barely peeking through the clouds I made my way to Pier 33. This city that I once loved was now a place I didn't want to be. It took a mere five days to not only change the way I saw San Francisco, but to change the way I saw people. My entire attitude toward life had changed and I felt that I had aged twenty years.

I thought about the time I spent with C.J. and a smile crept up on my face. I knew that C.J. was special; a kind man with a smile that I would always remember. He has a way of reaching into one's heart and not letting go. It was easy to understand why women flocked to him and I no longer found myself wondering how he was able to do that. People similar to C.J. seem to get through life using their looks to get what they want, but with C.J. it was different. He had charisma and it occurred to me that that was a rare quality these days.

I thought about Chuck and no matter how hard I tried I was unable to figure him out. At first glance it was apparent that he inherited his father's good looks, but his attitude and personality definitely came from somewhere else. I didn't like Chuck and after spending five days in San Francisco it was obvious that Chuck didn't like me either.

After all the letters I had received from C.J. I assumed I knew virtually all there was to know about him, but I had been wrong in my assumption. People are more than what they write in a few e-mail messages. They have lives, families and histories. I now know that it's our life experiences that make us who we are. I understood how C.J. became the man he became, but I wondered how Chuck became the man he came to be. What was it that happened in his life that made him so angry?

When it came to Chuck, C.J. had only one thing to say, *"It's good that he speaks his mind. Both he and Bella were raised to think for themselves, and whether I agree or disagree with their opinions, I respect them."* I wondered if C.J. really felt that way, or if it was the polite thing to say about one's own child. After much consideration I concluded that he really did feel that way.

Arriving at Pier 33 I glanced around and there he was; leaning up against the wall of Alcatraz Landing Café. My eyes shifted to the ground and I saw the shoebox. Chills ran down my spine and I momentarily considered running the other way. I wasn't sure whether or not I wanted it. Somehow I had the feeling that I was about to open Pandoras box and that may not be a good thing. Not that I wasn't interested in the contents of that box, but more because this family had taken an emotional toll on me and I wasn't quite sure how much more I could take.

I slowly approached him and when he noticed me he bent down and picked up the box. No words were spoken. The box was placed in my hands and I turned away.

Epilogue

The rain was steadily falling and the sound of thunder echoed throughout the room.

I sat down on the couch and pulled the throw blanket closer to my body. I felt chilled, understanding that it was a direct result of what was staring me in the face.

Four months had passed since my visit to San Francisco and I had not yet found the energy to look inside the box. After returning home I placed it on the top shelf of my closet and there it had remained until now.

C.J. had not mentioned the box, except to say *you will open it in time and when you do I trust that you will know what to do.* As I read those words they were eerily familiar. C.J. had written those very words in his goodbye letter. Of course, the letter was only a dream. The box however, was reality.

I sat there, staring at that box for a little more than an hour and it felt as if the box were staring back at me.

This is the first time I've heard anything about a box. What's inside the box?

My mother's life is inside this box.

Once again I felt the urge to run. My four month long attempt to avoid opening the box had come to an end and now I was faced with the fear of opening it.

Reaching my hand out, fully aware that it was trembling, I placed the box on my lap and slowly untied the red ribbon that had held the lid in place. Taking a deep breath, I slowly removed the lid and as I peered inside the box I felt the tears beginning to fill my eyes.

Chuck had not lied – this box did indeed hold his mother's life within it.

Hand still shaking, I removed the photo of Diana and momentarily wondered if she had placed the photograph in the box or whether C.J. had placed it there.

As I carefully removed the contents I silently began counting. In total there were eight journals, each containing more than two hundred and fifty hand written pages.

One by one I placed each journal on the table in front of me. Each was different in design; the first one that I picked up had a block style and was made of leather with an antique brass floral medallion on the front. The leather was worn and when I untied the strap and opened it a photograph greeted me. It was a photo of C.J. and Diana on their wedding day. I turned the page and began to read.